GOLD CAN

For Terry
Thanks to you
lovely wife
who I greatly
admire

[signature]

GOLDEN ^{THE} PELICAN

A Novel

GENE HELVESTON

MARLI BAR PRESS | INDIANAPOLIS

PUBLISHED BY MARLIBAR PRESSS

Acknowledgments: Thank you to my editor and designer, Mary Jo Zazueta, for her continued support and guidance.

MarLi Bar Press
Indianapolis, Indiana

Publisher's Cataloging-in-Publication Data

Names: Helveston, Eugene M., 1934- author.

Title: The golden pelican / Gene Helveston.

Description: First edition. | Indianapolis : MarLi Bar Press, [2017]

Identifiers: ISBN: 978-0-9972230-1-9 | LCCN: 2017910655

Subjects: LCSH: United States. Joint Chiefs of Staff—Officials and employees—Fiction | Korea (North)—Fiction. | Korea (North)—Politics and government—Fiction. | Intercontinental ballistic missiles—Korea (North)—Fiction. | United States. Central Intelligence Agency—Officials and employees—Fiction. | LCGFT: Political fiction. | Spy fiction. | Thrillers (Fiction) | BISAC: FICTION / Thrillers / Political.

Classification: LCC: PS3608.E39252 G65 2017 | DDC: 813/.6—dc23

Printed in the United States of America
First Edition

Cover and text design by Mary Jo Zazueta
tothepointsolutions.com

To the men and women of the
Central Intelligence Agency.

GOLDEN ^{THE} PELICAN

ONE

April 3, Monday

A S SOON AS THE SEAT BELT LIGHT WAS EXTINGUISHED, the passenger in 3-C unbuckled and rose from his seat. The collar of his overcoat was pulled up around his ears; not for the cold but to hide as much of his face as possible. He cradled a small carry-on bag, essentially a purse, under his left arm. It was the only luggage he had, and it was a comfort.

He was among the first half dozen passengers off the plane. Once he passed through the door, he hurried down the boarding ramp to reach the arrival area. The connections monitor overhead showed his next flight on Singapore Airlines would be departing from Gate 13. It was a short walk from Gate 6, where he was now standing.

Kang Bon-hwa would be in the air again within the hour. In another two hours, he would be a step closer to his final destination—known only to him. He was going to a place that was once the property of the Pope: Avignon, France.

_____

As Kang's plane approached Gate 6, two young women, Ko Min-jung and Yoo Hwa-yung, checked the photo they had been given of the passenger they were to meet. He was Korean; five feet, six inches tall; and said to be fifty-three years old. He was balding with stringy black hair that flowed along the sides. It was likely he would come off the plane with the first group of passengers because he was seated in first class.

When the fifth passenger off the plane entered the arrival area, the pair exchanged an unspoken nod of agreement. It was the man they would deal with.

Dodging the crush of departing passengers, Kang Bon-hwa headed left, as the women knew he would, toward Gate 13. After he had taken only a few steps, the two young women sidled up, one on each side of him. The woman on his left asked Kang where the flight he had just departed was from. As he turned slightly to answer her, the woman on his right, wearing a rubber glove on her right hand and holding a white cloth slightly dampened at the center, thrust the cloth over his nose and mouth for only a second before removing it with a wiping motion. Both women wheeled, separated, and proceeded at a normal pace in the opposite direction.

In less than three seconds, the cousin of the Supreme Leader of the Democratic People's Republic of Korea began reeling unsteadily and fell unconscious to the floor of the concourse. He died from respiratory and cardiac collapse in an ambulance on the way to the hospital, a victim of the most-deadly toxin existing today—VX.

———————

Only a few minutes before this event, the passenger in first-class seat 3-C, on a Koryo Airlines Tupolev Tu-204, nonstop from Pyongyang to Beijing, tidied up around his seat, put away his iPhone and ear buds, and retrieved his small carry-on from underneath the seat in front of him. The plane was on its final approach and would be landing in a matter of minutes. His connecting flight to Singapore was scheduled to depart in forty-five minutes. With only the one bag, the connection should be perfect. The gates for all international flights at Beijing Airport were in Terminal 3, and there was a possibility he would not be required to go through frontier inspection, the Chinese version of Customs and Passport control. Kang had planned ahead for this trip by shipping his most important belongings, life's essentials for him, from Pyongyang to Beijing, with directions to ship them to Singapore and from there, in a third leg to his final destination in France. With this triple pass, he was confident that his final destination would remain a secret.

The satchel he clutched contained fifty one-hundred dollar bills—"walking around money" for the trip—and the code for a Swiss bank safety deposit box that held one hundred thousand more. This was money Kang believed he deserved for the service he had given his country and for being a loyal family member. He was leaving North Korea because he was sure the country was doomed to certain destruction unless drastic steps were taken—and these steps were not in his power.

Planning for the trip began four weeks earlier after a

meeting Kang had with the Supreme Leader of the Democratic People's Republic of Korea, his cousin Kim Il-un. The diminutive and seemingly deranged Leader had confided in his cousin, which made Kang Bon-hwa nervous. He didn't want to know the information that was shared but there was no way for Kang to stop the Leader's drunken rant. This man, who lavishly spent the people's money on himself, did what he pleased, and listened to few people; possibly, he listened to no one. When Kim Il-un wanted to rant, he did. There was no stopping him. It was claimed that Kim spent as much as 600 million U.S. dollars each year while millions of his people lived in searing poverty. He lived his way; there was no other way for him.

Kang himself was no stranger to being a recipient of the unwitting largess of a country whose assets were absconded by a privileged few. As a member of the ruling family, Kang enjoyed a life that provided him comfort and demanded little in return. He was perfectly willing to live in this way, but the insane idea that North Korea could cow the most powerful nation on earth by launching a preemptive nuclear attack was madness. There could be no future for the country (or him) if this crazy plan was launched. The fact that his cousin had revealed the time and method of attack was dangerous information for Kang's health. His life could be in danger and there was no future for him at home.

With slurred speech, the Leader had bragged to his cousin about the successes that his missile program was achieving. "We can reach San Francisco today and, in the next few months, we will reach Denver!" he screamed. "Our goal is to light up the skies in the very heart of America with our own nuclear bomb. When these American fools feel the might of tiny Korea, they will be on their knees begging for mercy."

Kang was even more alarmed when the Leader continued.

"On the birth anniversary of our revered grandfather, the founder of the People's Republic, a full-scale attack will be launched against the United States. In 1950, we pushed the Americans and the other United Nations forces to the very tip of the Peninsula at Pusan. We should have driven them into the sea and won, but we faltered. This time, there will be no Inchon! We should take pride in the fact that Korea has already done to America what no one except our Vietnamese brothers have accomplished: fought the vast military forces of the United States to a draw. Remember, my dear cousin, we are still at war with our misguided brothers in the South. We must eliminate that vile regime and, at the same time, put those arrogant Americans in their place."

Kang had long since been removed from the political and military planning for the country and had essentially withdrawn to the role of private albeit privileged person because of his connections as a family member. Of course, the rant could have been just the drink talking, braggadocio, but it could also be a dangerous plan that the Leader intended to carry out.

From his days in the military inner circle, Kang knew that when it came to an event like this, the Supreme Leader would be close to the trigger that would launch the attack. Even if this made it harder to maintain secrecy, it would be how the Leader would carry out his plan. He would perform with flair in front of an audience. Keeping the details of time and place confidential and on an absolutely need-to-know basis would be crucial. But in a case like this, maintaining absolute secrecy would be difficult.

However, Kang knew the Leader had a unique advantage because his way of managing security was foolproof. If someone knew too much, or if a person displeased the Leader sufficiently, the remedy was simple: assassination.

The morning after this potentially life-threatening disclosure, Kang decided it was time to complete his plans for escape. He had been sending money regularly to Switzerland because he knew this day would come. It would be a pleasure to be re-united with his money. Ten million dollars would be sufficient for him to enjoy his exile in comfort and with security.

———————————

The morning after their meeting, the Supreme Leader woke with a headache and a vague memory of his indiscreet disclosure to a person who was no longer a close confidant or even part of the inner circle. Kim Il-un quickly put in motion the series of events that led to his cousin's fateful encounter with two young women in Beijing.

TWO

April 3, Monday

PHILLIP TRIPP SAT IN THE OVAL OFFICE BEHIND THE Resolute desk. Made from timbers of the *HMS Resolute*, a British ship salvaged by an American vessel and returned to the Queen of England as a token of friendship, many U.S. Presidents before Tripp had also sat there. The history was that a later Queen commissioned a desk to be made out of the wood and presented the desk to President Rutherford B. Hayes in 1880.

President Tripp derived a quiet pleasure and a measure of pride from the office he now held. By attaining this office, he was what many believed to be the single most-influential person in the world. Others would argue that the Pope held that distinction, and obviously when it came to spiritual matters and constituency, they would be right. But considering the billions of lives in every part of the world that could be affected by actions directed by the President of the United States, Phillip Tripp did have a heck of a big job. And there were the words his dad saddled him with the first time the younger Tripp was voted into office as a congressman: "No matter what rank or authority you have attained, it is not the *honor* bestowed on you that counts, it is the *responsibility* you assume for doing the right thing for the people you serve." His dad was right when he stressed this description of the servant leader.

It had been nearly four months since he had taken the oath of office. This put him beyond the artificial yardstick of the First 100 Days the media used to pump up ratings or readership. Things, so far, had gone reasonably well. His Cabinet was in place, and most of the lower-level supporting jobs for the Cabinet and the administration had been filled. Those who had valuable experience and were able to make the transition into the new administration were held over; the rest were new people who were both smart and suited to work hard while being loyal to their own boss and the President that they both served.

With a shock of prematurely white hair on top of a friendly face, the fifty-seven-year-old career politician was getting used to the responsibilities that went along with being the President of the United States. Having watched a spate of television shows that featured various goings on using a set that was an incredibly accurate copy of the office he now sat in, the President had a faux familiarity with his surroundings even before moving into the White House.

What happened in this room and, for that matter, *anything* he, as President, did or said, was like writing with indelible ink in a leaky boat. *Wow, how's that for a mixed metaphor?* the President thought. What he was thinking was there was no taking back anything. If it was said, it could become a headline—and it was out there. No matter how

often or how convincing the retraction, there was no eras-
ing something that had been spoken or, for that matter,
had been leaked as having been said! No matter how confidential or seemingly secure an occasion might seem, there
could always be a so-called anonymous leak to the press.

And how reporters loved to print a titillating quote,
credit it to an anonymous source, and then be willing to go
to jail, if necessary, to protect the source. When President
Tripp, in an off-hand remark in a private setting had said,
"The one thing that keeps me awake at night is the nuclear
threat from North Korea," the few people who had heard it
never would have leaked this comment to the press—but
they could have shared it with an aide; who shared it with
another aide; and, finally, someone far down the food chain
that is politics, made points with a reporter by becoming that
"reliable anonymous source 'close' to the White House."

After eight successful years in the U.S. House of Representatives, where he rose to chairman of Ways and Means;
two terms as Governor of Indiana; and ten years of teaching history and government at DePauw University, Phillip
Tripp felt like he had had a decent run of experience leading
up to this job. He realized he was labeled a career politician, which was not the sexiest of résumés in the present
political climate. But, after a war hero, a movie actor, a businessman, a peanut farmer, an oilman who owned a baseball
team and was the son of a former U.S. President, and finally
a philanderer—but not in that order—maybe it was time
to get back to the basics with a plain, old politician. After
all, some of the greatest leaders of the country had been
no more than career politicians. These included people
like John Adams (a loyal servant who crossed the Atlan-
tic Ocean twice to negotiate with European powers), James
Madison (who wrote the Bill of Rights), James Monroe (who
penned a doctrine banning European colonization in the
Western Hemisphere), Alexander Hamilton (who stabilized

the economy in time of crisis), and Abraham Lincoln (who preserved the Union and ended slavery). Of the Founding Fathers, George Washington and Thomas Jefferson could be labeled as hybrids.

Phil Tripp had been elected based mainly on his experience and expertise dealing with local and domestic issues. He won both the popular vote and the Electoral College, meaning most of the more than 200 million registered voters in the country were on his side. He won their support with his reasonable approach to management of the economy, controlling debt, and a sound approach to entitlements and healthcare. Some of his strongly held moral beliefs didn't necessarily endear him to the LGBT and Pro-Choice communities, but his impeccable record of honest dealing when it came to these and other contentious issues engendered disagreement not hate. No President could manage the broad range of domestic issues in a way that would suit everybody.

President Tripp believed that most Americans knew and appreciated right from wrong, and would be satisfied with a well-paying job, taxes that were reasonable and fair, a healthcare system that worked, and bridges that didn't fall down. And most of all, and almost entirely taken for granted, they wanted to be safe. He also knew that, except for the sad four years when Americans went about killing each other over the issue of secession in order to retain the stain of slavery; and in 1812, when the British made one last, futile attempt to tame their former colony, the country had been spared the bloodshed of war on its own soil. Protected east and west by vast oceans and north and south by nonthreatening neighbors, the people of this country, when at war, read about it in newspapers and saw events on their television and smart phones. Unless a loved one was lost or maimed in conflict, war was something that cost a lot of money but happened elsewhere and hurt someone else.

THREE

April 5, Wednesday

THE SUPREME LEADER SAT IN THE HELM OF HIS personal yacht which was secured alongside a carpeted wharf with two gangways that provided access. Kim was perched twelve feet above the main deck on the second of three levels of this 239-foot behemoth that weighed nearly 1,500 tons. The Feadship was built in the Netherlands in 2008, and was stationed in the Leader's private yacht basin at Wŏnsan. From his seat, the Supreme Leader could see the nearby palace and palatial grounds to his right, replete with its own amusement park, athletic fields, and guest houses; and to his left, across the bay, the airport where two jet aircraft and a helicopter were in waiting.

The dials on the console in front of the wheel and arrayed above a windshield that extended across the entire width of the helm station reported everything from the boat's location coordinates to the engine temperature and every other useful bit of information pertaining to the operation of a luxury yacht.

Kim loved being in this seat. The boat had accommodations for a crew of nineteen, although the number varied according to need. When the boat was being cleaned, which was a daily occurrence, and during times of maintenance, the deckhands numbered nearly a dozen. When entertaining a larger group, personal-service personnel numbered seven. The Captain, who supervised the activity of all of the crew except the cook and headwaiter, was aboard and at the helm any time the boat moved. At times when Kim was alone on the boat or entertaining privately, there were as few as five or six crew members and they were strictly confined to their quarters unless released by Kim.

When the boat was underway, Kim enjoyed steering, but felt secure only with the Captain at his shoulder. At times like this, with the boat securely docked, Kim enjoyed sitting in the helm seat. He made sure he was photographed as often as possible while in "action" at his station.

This yacht cost nearly 100 million dollars; it took as much as 700 thousand dollars to fill the fuel tanks, depending on the current price of fuel. Annual maintenance was more than five million dollars. If someone wanted to rent a boat like this, they would have to pay the handsome sum of one million dollars a week. Accommodations were limited to six privileged guests, making this possibly the most exclusive and expensive "hotel" in the world. The irony of an extravagance like this was lost entirely on Kim Il-un.

The Supreme Leader of the Democratic People's Republic of Korea (North Korea) was the third in what had become, by statute, a hereditary dynasty started with his grandfather and continued with his father. Kim lived in unbounded opulence in a country where many of the twenty-six million citizens starved. Exaggerated reports of North Koreans being six inches shorter in height than their South Korean counterparts spurred research on this possible difference. While the larger figure was refuted, current studies confirm that North Korean men are on average between 1.2 and three inches shorter than men in the South. Since there is essentially no genetic difference between the populations, this variance has to be real according to researchers. It has been decided the reduced stature is the result of chronic malnutrition that is especially detrimental when occurring in the first two years of life. They even predicted a never-before event would occur when the average South Korean woman would be taller than the average North Korean man. Another claim was that the brains of average North Koreans were likewise stunted, but this remains unsubstantiated.

The current leader was shorter and some say "dumber" and more likely out of touch with reality, compared to either his father or his grandfather. This begged the question: was this due to poor nutrition or was the Supreme Leader suffering from the effects of a unique lifestyle? A wag has quipped, "He will spend ten thousand for a bottle of wine, but is he eating his vegetables?" The answers were elusive because in the secret society Kim presided over, little was known about the thirty-three-year-old Leader, his family, or his personal life. All of this may be moot because whatever his deficiencies, the Leader held sway over his adoring population and was protected by loyal guards who knew that if the Leader deemed it necessary, any dissent would be stifled.

Kim enjoyed the company of a few loyal friends and a handful of benign family members. To stay in favor, all who dealt with Kim at any level were expected to maintain absolute loyalty. This started with listening and agreeing, and to be on the safe side, ultimately obeying. The Leader had no tolerance for dissent of any kind.

Kim, stationed at the helm, was anticipating his upcoming private meeting with one of his oldest and most loyal friends and relatives, General Lee Wu-jin, currently the Foreign Minister of the Democratic People's Republic of Korea. The general's late wife was a distant relative of the Leader's grandfather.

Even obscure relationships had significance in North Korean society and if there was any difficulty figuring out exact relationships, either uncle or cousin would do. Lee was younger than Kim's late father, but old enough to be an authority figure for the young Leader. Lee had been a dedicated political activist in his youth, and then he headed the post-Korean War military before assuming his current, purely political, role. In this position, Lee had occasion to visit the UN Headquarters in New York City several times. While there, he had befriended numerous high-level government officials from the U.S. and several European countries. Lee's exposure to Western life was rare for anyone from North Korea and it burdened him with ambiguity when it came to feelings for his home country.

As he approached the boarding ramp of the *Golden Pelican*, the Foreign Minister felt a foreboding that was almost palpable. He needed to shake it off before seeing Kim. Lee had had a good relationship with Kim's father. They dealt with each other as intellectual equals, but at the same time Lee was expected to acknowledge the authority of the elder Kim as the country's political leader, and he did so because failing this behavior would be at his own peril. Before that, Lee was in awe of the country's first Supreme Leader, who fought as a guerrilla aligning with the Communists and fighting the Japanese before Russia assumed control, by treaty, of North Korea after World War II.

Lee lamented the division of the peninsula and was envious of the stupendous growth enjoyed by the South, which had become economically and strategically aligned with the Western powers, especially the U.S. He was deeply saddened by the lack of prosperity and influence of his own Korea, under the rule of what was becoming an even more dysfunctional government. This was not something openly discussed, but Lee was sure he was not alone. This should be a topic that weighed on any loyal citizen of the North was Lee's feeling. He acknowledged, and was alarmed by, the remarkable progress of the South compared to the provincial backwardness that persisted in the North. Moreover, it was undeniable to Lee that the quality of leadership of his country had begun to erode with Kim Il-un's father and it was on an alarming decline with the current Leader. Kim's father had tried, but he was not able to lead the country forward using economic and political strategies. He skirted the strategy of conquest, never taking the final plunge. With Kim, all restraint seemed to have evaporated.

Paradoxically, as the capability of leadership in the country diminished, the aura of the Leader inexplicably approached near deity-like status—and that, Lee knew, promised disaster. The president of South Korea had recently been thrown out of office for corruption. Contrary to what most thought, Lee believed this was not a bad thing. It was good that citizens could employ a duly constituted court of law to determine if a government official was guilty of corruption. Then, if that person was guilty, he or she could be ousted and replaced by a new leader in a fair and democratic election process. A wrong was righted in the proper way by a citizenry with a voice.

At the head of the first flight of stairs taking him to the second deck, Lee paused to catch his breath. At his age, just over sixty, and being twenty pounds overweight, Lee Wu-jin was not as active as he had been in his army days. *It wasn't too late*, he thought. He should take more care with his diet and get more exercise. At the top of the next flight, Lee spotted Kim gazing ahead as he sat in the helmsman's seat, looking like a child playing make-believe. Every time he saw this fool, as he appeared now in this ridiculous charade, new concerns arose in Lee's mind. Where would the antics of this man lead their country? How much longer could his bragging and threats of nuclear attack be contained? Would it be possible to convince Kim that the only power imparted by nuclear capability was simply having it, not using it? Once nuclear force is unleashed, as it was for the first time during World War II, its leverage as a strategic weapon is lost. When a nuclear weapon is used by one country against another country that also has nuclear capability, it could lead to their mutual destruction. It had never happened. Yet. Because based on this premise, no person in their right mind would unleash such a weapon, especially against a country like the United States.

Lee believed with all of his heart in the truth of what he had heard from the United States Ambassador to the UN on his first visit to America: The only legitimate uses of nuclear energy are to create energy and prevent war.

The atomic bomb used at the end of World War II, most experts believed, ended the war several months earlier than it would have otherwise ended and saved from hundreds of thousands to more than a million lives, both civilian and military. The bombs were dropped only after Japanese citizens were warned that a device more powerful than any ever used in war might be dropped on cities with military significance. Citizens were warned to flee in advance of the attack, but there was no mass removal of the population in response to these warnings. Some people at the time, and others today, have criticized the United States for not providing a more effective warning by detonating a sample blast on an uninhabited island—but that option was not available in 1945, thereby making the suggestion moot.

With the horrific events at Hiroshima and Nagasaki, where a combined 125,000 people were killed and more than a dozen square miles reduced to rubble, the world had its warning—and it needed no further evidence of the destructive power of a nuclear detonation.

FOUR

April 5, Wednesday

"HELLO, UNCLE!" CALLED THE LEADER OVER HIS shoulder when he saw Lee's reflection in the glass above the console. Lee cringed inside at the familiar and familial greeting.

He answered with a generic, "My best wishes to you, my Leader. Your vessel is as impressive as ever. And, if I do say so, it looks bigger and grander every time I see it. Am I shrinking? Is your boat growing? Or is my memory simply fading and being taken over by fantasy?" Not expecting an answer, the Foreign Minister continued. "It is always good to see you; especially here, on the boat that we both love."

The boat was nice but that was not the only reason Lee enjoyed being there. It was a relief to be spared the oppressively heavy and overdone combination of ornate-gold, wooden-framed Russian chairs with garishly upholstered seats and backs that were awkwardly mixed with native oriental scrolls; ornate, carved, wooden furniture in the local style; and the heavy scent of the perfume and incense that surrounded Kim in his palace. The clean Western lines and functionality of this magnificent vessel, which far outshone its owner, were a welcome respite for Lee's senses that had undeniably become aligned with Western tastes.

Turning in his seat to face the Minister, Kim Il-un continued the banter. "You look as you always have to me, Uncle. Maybe a little thicker in the middle, but you continue to be your same old self."

Even that banal comment was above grade, even urbane, for the usually dull and concrete Kim, thought Lee. "Is there any special issue you want to discuss, Leader? Your message just requested this meeting without any other directions for me. I don't have any ready answers for a specific request you might have, but your old uncle can still think on the fly." The Minister lightened up a bit with his response. Lee knew there was never anything to be gained with Kim if there was even a hint of opposition or confrontation or for that matter any utterance that could possibly be misunderstood and received with umbrage.

"To be honest, Uncle, there is," said Kim.

"I am at your disposal. Let me hear what you wish to share with me," said Lee with an indulgent smile. Lee worried it was obvious he was only pretending that he thought what Kim said made sense and that he was complicit in whatever scheme he might come up with. *Will he brag about eliminating Cousin Kang Bon-hwa in such a disgraceful and public manner as he did, but is stoutly denying? Can he possibly know how alarmed I am and how horrified I will be when he tells me what I think is on his mind?* The Foreign Minister did not have long to wait.

"The time is now," snorted Kim. "The President in the U.S. is new and untested. No other country in the West besides America has the stomach to deal with us. The people of the Middle East have their own problems, and anything we accomplish that would increase the power and influence of our country at the expense of the United States can only please our friends and supporters in Russia and China. We will be the only people with the courage and stamina to put the world right and, in the bargain, we can straighten out the problems coming from division within our own country." Kim paused, as much to let his words sink into his own mind as for the benefit of his guest. He was not done. "And, my dear Uncle, when I say 'our country,' I mean from the Yalu River to Pusan. Our country is not North and South—it is Korea and it belongs to those who are resourceful and independent and not dogs that live off the leavings of the West.

"There are twenty-eight thousand foreign soldiers in the South, and that means our cousins in the South are not free. They are occupied. It is no different now than it was with the Japanese. The South bends to the will of a foreign power. Their population is subjected to the tastes of the plundering hordes who invaded our peninsula nearly seventy years ago and who remain in significant numbers today."

It was not clear to Lee if Kim actually believed that the Americans had invaded Korea—a myth that was perpetuated in the country based on decades of purposeful misinformation. This would certainly be at odds with Kim's pride in his grandfather, who started the war. The goal of the original Supreme Leader was to unify the country and establish Communist ideology as practiced in the North. He nearly succeeded. Kim wanted to have it both ways and there was nobody to contradict him.

Continuing his diatribe, Kim summed up his opinion of the South. "They ship fancy cars, computers, and phones with cameras, but it is only to support their own decadent lifestyle and to gain favor with their conquerors and occupiers. It is time for us to act. We can put off our obligation no longer."

His emotional outburst spent, Kim assumed a conspiratorial visage as he prepared to finally reveal his specific plans. "My beloved Uncle and Minister, we are one of nine countries in the world possessing nuclear warheads. We are, by far, the smallest, but just having this weapon means that when it comes to nuclear might we are no less powerful than countries more than ten times our size—and there is more in our favor. Adding the billion plus combined population of our allies in Russia and China, and the billions of Muslims that the West has alienated, the weight of numbers of people is on our side. The time is right for us to act now."

With this, a head appeared in the forward passageway that led to the crew's quarters. A young man, appearing to be just beyond the teen years, peeked out. Kim cast a brief and disapproving look and the head immediately withdrew. The face was vaguely familiar to Lee. He had seen the boy before, but where?

"For us to succeed, we must coordinate our efforts by striking both the South and the heart of the United States simultaneously. The first part, attacking the South, will be easy." His eyes glazed over and his speech became more rapid as Kim went on." My generals tell me our 170-millimeter self-propelled Koksan guns with rocket-assisted projectiles can easily reach Seoul's twenty-five million population. They can deliver five hundred thousand rounds in the first hour. This attack will kill a half million people and will paralyze that city and, in effect, the entire country.

"At the same time, we will launch a nuclear warhead on a new Losan intercontinental missile. Our choice for a target is either San Francisco or Denver. An attack on either city would be sufficient to deliver our message, but the effect would be even more devastating if we hit them at the very middle of the country. This would deliver a message to the Americans that there is nowhere in their country that a person can feel safe. We may even strike both cities.

"The third arm of our attack will start with a message to Japan. If they take no action and are willing to maintain normal diplomatic relations with Korea—that is, the *entire* peninsula unified as the Democratic People's Republic of Korea—we will forgive them for their years of subjecting us to the level of a mere colony. We can be friends, but on our terms. Any hostile response on their part will be met with a devastating attack. They will not be told what it will be, but our use of a nuclear weapon for the Americans will make it clear that Japan could receive the same. This close to home, the use of conventional weapons would be my first choice, but our delivery systems are not sufficient to deliver a punishing blow that far away, so it may be necessary to carry out a nuclear attack on our island neighbors.

"I will tell just you, Uncle, I don't believe the people of Japan have the stomach for another nuclear attack and I believe they will bend to our wishes."

The Minister remained silent and listened attentively until it was clear that the Leader was finished speaking. "Kim ..." He purposely dropped the deferential manner that was flattery not respect. "What you propose leaves no provision for a fallback if things don't proceed immediately as planned. Are we underestimating the will of the West?" Lee's aim was to stress that he was speaking as an older and more experienced man talking with someone who he had watched grow up from a toddler.

Before anything more could be said, Kim Il-un held up his hand to hush the older man. "Nuclear force as a deterrent is useful only to those who are already strong," he said. "This power accomplishes nothing more than allowing them to use other force to maintain a world where the economic and political might of the West continues to rule. Only those who have the potential for destruction of others can enslave the weak, take territory from the rightful owner, and monopolize markets simply because they can get away with it."

This last comment was scarier to Lee than much of what he had previously heard. The Leader was offering what sounded like well thought out and logical reasons for his proposed actions, even if they were the unfulfillable wishes of an ideologue. What he said was not a convincing argument that he could succeed, but it did provide his reasoning. Should the Minister introduce the concept to the Leader that the people he wanted to destroy were directed by something that he had no knowledge or understanding of, something called a *moral compass*? Lee, being honest with himself, recognized that having this guidance did not always make people right. But, he had come to truly believe the aims of those who honor morality, for the most part, is the result of trying to accomplish that which is for the greater good. The actions of people in a truly democratic society are not always in concert. Although well-meaning, they can sometimes be blurred by a lack of agreement about the best methods to employ even though the desired end result is the same. *Kim leads a country he calls a "democratic" republic when it is actually the antithesis of democracy.* Would Lee's words fall on the deaf ears of a person who has no ability to comprehend? They probably would, but Lee decided to finish what he had started.

Lee decided the best way to proceed would be to tell the young Leader what happened after World War II. "After the great war of the mid-twentieth century," he began, "people were astounded at the behavior of the victorious United States. Trading commerce for war, the victorious Americans provided funds to begin re-building war-ravaged countries, and this included its allies and its former enemies whose nonbelligerent population were now considered friends. Then the Americans sponsored a policy of free trade that enabled the unfettered exchange of goods and services between all countries. Then, to ensure that safe delivery routes were available everywhere, the United States maintained the only navy with worldwide coverage. This was not pure charity. The better the rest of the world did, the better it was for the United States.

"This was a perfect example to the world of a win-win proposition. For those former enemies, this behavior was unheard of—and set a new standard." This recitation led Lee to offer a comment that actually came to him for the first time as he was speaking these words. "My dear Leader," he said, "I will leave you with the following advice, which I believe with all my heart. It is this: The best country to have for a friend is also likely to be the very worst to have as an enemy."

FIVE

April 10, Monday

THE PRESIDENT LEFT THE OVAL OFFICE ON HIS WAY TO the 5,500-square-foot complex that made up the Situation Room on the ground floor in the West Wing. *It should be rooms*, he thought, *because in addition to the main conference room, several smaller venues were included in the major renovation completed in 2007.* One of these smaller rooms was his choice for today's meeting.

The news from North Korea was not good. Last week Kim Il-un had conducted another missile test, and in the past eighteen months they detonated two underground nuclear devices, their fourth and fifth. Their success had been marginal, but even so, any country with nuclear capability and a method for delivery was a threat. Moreover, it had become apparent the North Koreans were being aided by the Iranians who were willing to trade their missile technology for help from North Korea with the actual building of a bomb.

More than quarter of a century after receiving four billion dollars in food and energy aid from the U.S., in return for a promise to freeze and gradually dismantle its nuclear weapons, North Korea continued unabated with its program to develop nuclear weapons and build missiles to deliver them. In retrospect, this was not a deal that went sour. It was one that was sour from the beginning. The United States had given them a big prize upfront and received only a promise that was never kept. *You don't start your kid's meal with Twinkies and expect him to eat his spinach. Oops, I did it again*, thought the President. *Better slow down on the homey analogies.*

The meeting this morning was an introductory session and was scheduled to last just an hour. There would be no need to share today's discussion widely among his staff or to seek opinions from anybody but the most knowledgeable and trusted of his advisors. In attendance would be key members of his national security team: Vice President Phyllis Landane, Secretary of Defense Al Teague, Chairman of the Joint Chiefs of Staff General William Wieland, Director of National Intelligence Orville McPherson, National Security Advisor D. L. Provisor, Homeland Security Advisor General Forrest Elder, Ambassador to the United Nations Miki Haldon, and Chief of Staff Chris Kristofferson.

The dark-walnut paneling on three walls of the small room was complemented by a fourth wall of textured light-tan wallpaper. There were two large rectangular windows on this wall, located just above eye level. In the windows, the tint was slight but the bullet proofing was substantial. The view of trees outside provided welcome relief from the otherwise cloistered atmosphere of this intimate room. Around the twelve-foot polished wooden table, with the President at the head, the eight other participants were seated. There were no name cards or department designations; something usually reserved for larger gatherings, including cabinet meetings and others that included ancillary staff. This meeting would be short, focused, and private. This was a new administration and people were just beginning to get comfortable with each other. In these circumstances, it was natural for the President to assemble his closest advisors, most of whom would be wrestling with a problem as serious as today's for the first time. Actually, the situation was the same for the President, but he felt especially good about this group.

"The chickens have come home to roost when it comes to North Korea," was the President's opening comment to the men and women around the table. He continued, "The sad part is, we may be doing the same thing in the Middle East with Iran." He was referring to action just completed that was similar to when the United States first tried to limit nuclear proliferation on the part of North Korea in 1994. As the U.S. did then, once again our country had concluded a nuclear nonproliferation agreement with an antagonistic government with payment upfront and results expected later. The recent deal with Iran started with the U.S. lifting crippling decade-long sanctions that were aimed at thwarting the de-stabilizing effect of Iran's nuclear ambitions. Then, we freed 1.5 billion dollars in frozen assets, and sweetened the pot with four hundred million dollars in cash delivered on pallets as ransom payment for our sailors who were recently abducted contrary to international law and were treated in violation of the Geneva Convention.

This largess was based on a promise that Iran would merely slow, not stop, development of nuclear warheads for ten years. After that time, it would be a virtual certainty that Iran would have weapons-grade uranium to arm nuclear warheads. At the same time Iran would be promising to slow uranium enrichment they would be given the privilege of self-inspection. In addition, they would not be required to recant or even soften their vow to annihilate neighboring Israel. To make the deal even worse, there would be no lessening of Iran's continuing support for international terrorism. These chickens were still out, but sure to come back to haunt us—probably sooner rather than later.

The President continued, "We are all aware of the incessant saber rattling of the North Koreans, not only their rhetoric but also undeniably dangerous acts: five underground nuclear tests, the latest in 2016, and ongoing missile tests with the aim of perfecting a missile that has intercontinental range and the ability to carry a sizable nuclear warhead. Their nuclear and long-range delivery aspirations have been made perfectly clear to the world. In addition, in terms of conventional arms, they have the ability to unleash a devastating artillery barrage on the city of Seoul. In this attack alone, it is estimated that 500,000 people would be killed and untold damage would be inflicted on the city and the entire nation. Now, I would like to hear from you."

Nodding to the Director of National Intelligence (DNI), the President gave the table to Orville McPherson, a tall, serious African American. As DNI, McPherson was boss of the head spy, the Director of the Central Intelligence Agency. Getting right to the point, the Director, who was a man who didn't mince words, said, "I have to tell you right now that we have a big problem facing us, or, I should say, we have problems. There are two. First, as we all know, and the President has already reminded us, a rogue regime in North Korea is on the brink of being able to deliver a nuclear warhead to virtually anywhere in the world. The second is that this activity is taking place in a closed society that has been and continues to be extremely difficult to penetrate. That is not to say that we don't have assets on the inside, but even those who are there have definite limitations. Even working as close to the edge as possible, the very inner circle has been impossible for our team on the ground to crack. We have a good idea of the big picture. It tells us that North Korea will be able to launch a nuclear warhead soon, and that the ruler would like to do just that. The question is this: is Kim crazy enough to trade the minutes or hours of satisfaction he would get from inflicting pain on the U.S. for the certain and total annihilation of his own country? In my opinion, our best chance of success is to resist the impulse to outgun him and instead thwart the Leader's ambitions by working from the inside, and then hope that cooler heads will prevail and take over the governance of the country."

"A regime change?" questioned Chief of Staff Chris Kristofferson.

"You could call it that," McPherson responded.

General Forrest Elder said, "We all know that assassination is off the books, but how likely is it that there will be enough sensible people close enough to the seat of power to get Kim Il-un out of the picture and replace him with a democratic government? How serious are these folks about the dynastic succession? This current fellow is the third. Is there anyone in the wings?"

Vice President Landane, who had the reputation of being an academic, read from a typed sheet of paper. "Clause 2 of Article 10 of the Ten Fundamentals of the Korean Workers Party states that the party and the revolution must be carried out eternally by the Baekdu bloodline. This family began with the grandfather, who fought the Japanese in 1945 and who later started the Korean War. That was in 1950, and it attempted to re-unify Korea. He was succeeded by his son and now his grandson Kim Il-un, the present leader, who is said to be married and have a daughter. He is more extroverted than his father and grandfather but his stated aspiration to present the image of an academic who is more masculine, seems to have fallen well short of attainment—no pun intended. He looks like he is not more than five feet five inches tall, and maybe even less."

During a brief pause, the President noted Al Teague and General Wieland with their heads together. This seemed to be a natural alignment between Defense and the Joint Chiefs. Looking at them, the President said, "Your thoughts, gentlemen."

The body language between the men indicated that General Wieland, Chairman of the Joint Chiefs of Staff, would do the talking. "Mr. President," he began, "our options are well defined, clearly different, and anything but ideal based on the predicament that we face."

"Bad as the options might be, General, let's hear what you two have cooked up," said the President.

"For a start, Mr. President, we could strike preemptively; delivering one or more nuclear devices from aircraft flying from a base in Japan. Our current B-2 Stealth Bomber would be the tactical choice. The bombs would be W76 100-kiloton-TNT equivalent class. This would be a bomb with ten times the power of the first nuclear bomb used in Hiroshima. Our total nuclear arsenal now numbers 4,500 units. They range from low-energy tactile warheads with 0.01 kiloton TNT equivalents to those with nine thousand kilotons and we have tested weapons to fifteen thousand kilotons. In my opinion, and I don't hold this alone, such an action would profoundly change the world as we know it. If such an attack took place, I believe that we would be on our own. I doubt that any other nation would back us, even if they were ultimately glad that we did it. Even with North Korea neutralized, seven other countries besides the United States have nuclear capability. There is no way to predict the eventual outcome of our striking first. We do not favor this plan."

"Pretty grim, General. What else?" said the President.

"Conventional, nonnuclear war. That is, a strike using

conventional arms could be carried out with devastating effect," continued General Wieland, "but it would require a massive concentration of warships, most likely in the Sea of Japan. This level of preparation would definitely tip our hand, eliminating any chance of surprise, and would undoubtedly lead to a response from both Russia and China. They would match our buildup with ships of their own, and who knows what else? We would have a messy situation on our hands that would find us in a collision course with both China and Russia. This is something we believe simply can't be done. A pre-emptive strike on our part would be technically unprovoked; that is, by definition. But that begs the question, how do we deal with repeated threats from an absolute leader who has nuclear weapons and a means to deliver them and who we know is impulsive and uncontrolled?

"What constitutes provocation? We know Israel has been living under the threat of attack from a country just a thousand miles away. The Israelis have actually carried out preemptive conventional arms strikes against Iranian nuclear facilities without retaliation while receiving the tacit approval of most of the rest of the world—but is action like this possible in the situation we face? We know from the Israelis that living under threat is possible, but why should a country put up with this and how long should a nation wait before one of these threats is carried out against them, especially when it is a nuclear threat? Finally, this is the first time in history that such a threat has been leveled by a country that has nuclear capability against a country that also has this capability. My conclusion is that if we don't deal with the North Koreans now, it is virtually guaranteed this will happen with Iran in a decade.

"We have created this problem by kicking the can down the road, and who knows how much cheating the Iranians are doing? The ten-year timeline could be both artificial and inaccurate. Based on what we know of their activities, the Iranians could have a bomb much sooner. In that case, we would have the North Korea situation all over again. To add fuel to the fire, with Iran, we are dealing with a country that is far ahead of North Korea when it comes to missile technology, and there is evidence that Iran is helping North Korea perfect its missile delivery systems. Both countries are led by ideologues and both countries have vowed to attack another sovereign country. We should deal with the North Korean threat now and set the standard for behavior of countries that could pose a nuclear threat in the future." With this, the Chairman sat back and listened.

This was a long oration for a meeting like this, but it was a necessary one, the President felt.

Vice President Phyllis Landane spoke next. "How about traditional diplomacy?"

"Thank you, Phyllis," said the DNI. "That was to be my next point. This kind of thing is not what I do, but my guess is that the situation has gotten beyond the talking stage, and an all-out military strike is all but ruled out. The President did a great job getting the Chinese to withhold coal supplies and food support, but will this be a deterrent or a provocation in itself?"

"We can get Russia and China on board and simply out wait them," offered Miki Haldon, the UN Ambassador. Her comment didn't sound like it convinced even herself.

The gaze of the Director of National Intelligence panned the group and then settled on the President at the head of the table. "Mr. President, I realize our options aren't good. I think we can all agree on that. I haven't overlooked the defensive posture of intercepting a missile with our own devices, but this, to me, is only a last-ditch option. Even a 99 percent success rate isn't satisfactory when it comes to a nuclear warhead. I am not trying to drum up business for our own agency, but it seems that some type of covert action is called for. We can't kill the Leader ourselves, but we can find people in the regime and close to the Leader who would do what is necessary to obtain power and pursue an approach that would be good for both countries. We have assets in place in North Korea and we have sufficient backup in the South, but no specific plan is currently in place. There may be a role for the Central Intelligence Agency, but we simply don't have concrete plans in motion at this time."

"Thank you, all," said the President. "Most of you have had something to say, and I assume that those of you who did not speak are more or less in agreement with what has been discussed. We have a problem. We can eliminate this problem, but with the surest option, a nuclear attack, the price could be too high because of collateral damage." He thought of the time he smashed a spider on the back of his wife's new white blouse. He successfully eliminated the threat but left an ugly red splotch—collateral damage. He kept this thought to himself. "I will continue to communicate with the Chinese Premier. He has been reasonable, and I believe he thinks it is more important to maintain good trade relations with the United States than to prop up the regime of Kim Il-un; not to mention I truly believe he is categorically opposed to the use of nuclear force. With the complicated issues in Syria and their connections to Iran, Russia may not be approachable when it comes to North Korea, but the option of cooperating with the Russians is still on the table.

"This group will meet again on Friday. I look forward to hearing from anyone in the meantime who can further our planning." With that, the President rose and headed back to the Oval Office.

"A man of few words," General Wieland said of the President. His comment was meant for Orville McPherson as the two made their way out of the Situation Room. He had not had any personal dealings with the DNI, but from what he had seen of him in the meeting, he seemed like a capable man. The General was convinced that the problem with North Korea would be dealt with best from the inside and that meant by using spies.

"Yup," responded Orville, a man of fewer words.

SIX

April 10, Monday

MAJOR ADAM GRANT, ONLY A FEW WEEKS INTO HIS post as Adjutant to four-star General William Wieland, waited for his boss to return from the hastily called meeting with the President and other members of the national security team. This was a good time for the young major to review the world situation as he saw it relating to his boss, himself, and the work they had ahead of them.

North Korea's latest missile launch was a huge success for Kim Il-un. The missile had delivered a payload equal to a five-megaton nuclear warhead, five thousand and five hundred nautical miles from its launch—the distance from Pyongyang to Denver. In a futile attempt to downplay the test, the missile was directed toward Antarctica, with instruments onboard to record the distance traveled and then to destroy it after a predetermined distance. Technicians from seven nations, including the United States, had tracked the missile from shortly after takeoff to its destruction. There are no secrets in space.

The Russians had taken over the Ukrainian Federation of Crimea, and their efforts to dominate the entire country were moving ahead deliberately. Using coercion and thuggery, aided by the protective indifference of the UN, Russia was on its way to re-establishing a Stalin-like era under the leadership of the elected President Vladimir Putin, who was, in actuality, a dictator. He had been at the seat of power for more than seventeen years.

Iran was only a few years away from "guaranteed" nuclear capability for use in war. It continued to test intermediate and long-range missiles, and had placed a sixteen-billion-dollar order for eighty Boeing jets, including fifteen 777-9s, the world's largest commercial airliner capable of accommodating four hundred passengers or a lot of other cargo. All of this was the result of an ill-conceived, but politically expedient "treaty" by the U.S. Government in the name of the Chief Executive. It was done this way because the agreement had no chance of passing in the Senate, the only government body that can ratify a treaty.

Peace in the Middle East was as remote as always. Only Israel and Jordan, under a courageous and informed leader, demonstrated anything near common sense, and that included only the power players. Africa remained a quagmire of poverty and internecine slaughter bordering on genocide. Governments throughout Latin America struggled with corruption and instability. China strived for hegemony in Asia while ignoring anything but her own political wishes; only bending to the most extreme of economic pressures. In our hemisphere, a Chinese company with close ties to Beijing owned ports at both ends of the

Panama Canal, while the U.S. military guaranteed neutrality and safety for this waterway. The jury was still out on this "deal."

Major Adam Grant a West Point graduate and veteran of two tours in Afghanistan was surprised by his appointment as Adjutant to the Joint Chiefs of Staff, the principal military advisor to the President of the United States. But after the General explained the reasons for Adam's selection, it made more sense.

"I chose you for several reasons," the General told Adam his first day on the job. "I was impressed by your record at West Point. It takes some brains to perform as well as you did on the debate team, and being captain of the golf team when you aren't low man tells me you are a good leader. You probably had the size and ability to do well on the football team, but I am glad you avoided this and spared your noggin from all the abuse it could have taken. You look like a guy who is not afraid to lead with his head, and I like that, but not on the gridiron! I was also impressed with your work in Afghanistan. You led troops and you did a whale of a job on the administrative end of things. I believe you have what it takes to do this job but ..." The general, who had been at his post for only four months admitted, "Major, we both have a lot to learn."

The general shared most of what was happening at the higher levels of government as it pertained to the military with Adam, and Adam accompanied General Wieland to larger meetings, although there was much more that happened in smaller meetings and even in hallway conversations. The general stressed the difference between policy and strategy. "Elected officials, the 'politicals,' and their handpicked staff decide what they hope to achieve. This is policy. These policy decisions can be influenced by the input of advisors, including military advisors like me, but policy is political and usually originates with a campaign promise. These promises are merely statements of an intention to produce results. These results are attained only through action. This action depends on strategy, which is the plan, and tactics, which embody the action required. We, in the military, are for the most part simply informed when it comes to policy; we have some influence, but not much. When it comes to how this policy is carried out, strategically and tactically, we have a big responsibility—that is our job. The way I see it, the policy of our nation is to be safe now and to remain so, and the strategy and tactics employed to accomplish this when diplomacy fails is the responsibility of the military."

Adam was impressed by how General Wieland simplified the process while respecting the magnitude of the job and the importance of the players in the game.

The General continued, "When diplomacy and reasoning fail, especially when it comes to foreign affairs, simply surviving may depend on the use of force. This force can be exercised in one of two ways. By far the best way to use force is to simply threaten to use it, and you can do this only if you actually have it. Ronald Reagan employed this strategy brilliantly in his multiple face-offs with several leaders of the Soviet Union. He won the Cold War for the United States without firing a shot.

"Then, there is the actual use of force. Military action. The best example of this is what the United States accomplished in World War II. A country initially leaning toward isolationism was provoked into building the most effective fighting machine ever assembled. This force was then used to vanquish Imperial Japan and Hitler's Germany because we had the best people and material." The General leaned back in his chair, surveyed the room, and looked squarely at his aide. "Sorry to pontificate, Adam, but saying all of this out loud helps me too."

Adam responded, "General, this helped me a lot. I kind

of knew most of what you just said already, but it is nice to have it explained in a clear and logical way. I look forward to the challenges ahead. I have confidence in you and, when it comes to you doing your job, I hope that I can be of some help and earn your confidence in me."

Adam Grant's new job was both a dream and a nightmare. At best, he was enjoying a hot dog at the ballgame and at worst he was watching sausage being made—net good but not all good.

Dream job or nightmare, Adam lived with the memory of an unspeakable event that took place in mid-Ohio three years earlier. A crazed terrorist, following the dictates of a radical mullah, used his car as an instrument of death and careened down a sidewalk in a quiet college town, snuffing out the life of Adam's fiancée and seriously injuring four other students. Then the perpetrator got his wish: he was gunned down by Campus Security and, according to a myth that he believed, he died a martyr and was met by virgins in the afterworld.

Adam had met Amy Hollings five years earlier at Dennison University in Granville, Ohio, when she was a senior studying political science and he was on campus to speak at an assembly of ROTC students from the more than a dozen schools in the state that offered an ROTC curriculum. A new Captain and West Point graduate home from a tour in Afghanistan, the ruggedly handsome soldier in a six-foot frame was exactly the image the U.S. Army wanted to present to the eager, young ROTC candidates. Adam's talk with the students went well, but having a blind date with the smartest and most beautiful woman he had ever met eclipsed all. This blind date turned into a cross-country romance, with a nearly equal division of travel time, and culminated in a proposal of marriage after two years.

While Adam returned to Afghanistan for his second tour, Amy decided to pursue her doctorate and take on a job at Dennison University as a teaching assistant. The wedding would happen when Adam had a reasonable chance of being home. Amy died just two months before that date.

Amy's death cruelly deprived him of what could have been. After this loss, Adam extended his tour in Afghanistan, after which he was assigned to his present job. He had spent nearly five years in one of the longest deployments for anyone serving in this operation.

Even in the rush of his job as Adjutant, thoughts of Amy remained. His volunteering for an extended tour in Afghanistan actually helped Adam cling to his sanity. After that tour, he knew he was not suicidal. He had lived in a place where death was a possibility around any corner. And he had survived. Amy would have expected nothing less.

Working at a much higher level than he had ever imagined possible this early in his career, Adam was looking forward to the challenges. These would present a different brand of 'combat.' His arms now would be intellectual prowess and persistence, new ways of meeting challenges that would fill his hours as he dealt with the underpinnings of his lingering grief. He would employ a single-minded focus on this important job. He knew Amy, who was the kind of person who would be better at preventing war than waging it, would be proud of what he was now doing.

Adam had already rationalized his belief system. Oxymoronically he embraced what he called "secular religiosity." Adam spent twelve years being educated in Catholic schools, and for the first eight years began every Wednesday morning attending Mass with his schoolmates. He believed in God and the redemptive powers of the sacrifice of Jesus Christ, but his mind was logical and guided by scientific truths—which put him in a belief system where he teeter-tottered between the mystical and the concrete.

He had not shared these thoughts with anyone. He never would. Adam was comfortable in himself. He envisioned his role in life as something like being a guard at the Tomb of the Unknown Soldier—total dedication and singleness of purpose—but in a different direction. He wanted to do more than maintain a spotless uniform and complete the twenty-one steps in perfect form repetitively while wearing moistened white gloves to better grip his gun.

Adam, like anyone who followed the news and read serious books, was fully aware of the imminent danger for a world that contained more than 17,000 nuclear warheads in nine countries. Of those countries, two were dishonest and unprincipled and one was led by an unbalanced despot. One third were bad apples. The other six did not always agree, and they may even violently disagree on some issues, but they were restrained by the certainty that nuclear war would mean mutual destruction.

Of the three countries that were especially dangerous: Pakistan was governed by a combination of religious zealots and corrupt politicians who provided a safe haven for terrorists; Russia was led by a dictator who maintained control at home by terror and threat and sought expansion by force at his borders; and North Korea was led by a deranged parricide who was openly threatening the United States with nuclear attack.

Adam admitted to himself that he may be over-committed to doing something useful, but he was sane. He was a patriot who grew up inspired by the words of Patrick Henry: "Give me liberty or give me death." These were a guide, even though he later learned Henry was a loquacious gadfly who was a pain in the neck for the more effective patriots, our Founding Fathers. Adam's concerns were only intensified as he listened to General Wieland say that the thing that was most likely to keep the President awake at night was the nuclear threat from North Korea. When the General described conditions as he saw them, Adam's concerns remained but were even better focused. The General made it clear that U.S. policy to discourage North Korea's ambitions to wage nuclear war was clear and well-founded. The problem we faced now was that this policy was not yet backed by a strategy or tactics to be employed; something that concerned the President and his national security advisors.

What would George Washington do if he were alive today? Adam thought. The father of our country answered the call to action in 1775 when he left Mount Vernon to lead the continental army to victory over the British in a war that took six years, and whose outcome was never certain up to the end. *It is inconceivable*, Adam thought, *that a patriot like George Washington would be sitting on his hands if he were here today. He would do something, but could he act in the name of a government as it exists today the same way he did in a country held together only a with a loose confederation?* Not likely was Adam's conclusion. *Does this mean nothing this heroic can be done today because of the complexity of our government, or does it mean that the country can be protected only by something or someone acting outside of, but at the same time for, the Government and the people?*

SEVEN

April 11, Tuesday

T HE PHONE IN THE OUTER OFFICE RANG. CISSY FRIEND said, "Yes, I will" and pressed a button to alert General William Wieland, her new boss, that the call was for him. Cissy was a holdover from the previous Chairman, retained because she was loyal, smart, and overtly apolitical. She put the call through without the usual, "I will see if the General is available." It was Orville McPherson, Director of National Intelligence. Cissy knew that the General was available and would definitely want to hear from the Director.

Cissy had been around long enough to sense the tension that everyone was working under. She read the newspapers and watched the news on television, mostly Fox, but she also listened to the left-leaning broadcast channels on Sunday mornings. Going to mass on Saturday allowed her to do this in good conscience. She flipped through channels and watched MSNBC and CNN during the week, just so she couldn't be labeled as totally drinking the Kool-Aid.

She couldn't remember a time when things were as dicey as they were now; especially with North Korea. Cissy was only six when the Cold War ended in 1991. She imagined things were as tense then as they were now. She thought of the long-ago Cuban Missile Crisis, which she had only read about. *That must have been a humdinger*, she thought.

"General, this is Orville McPherson." His voice was melliferous, even in the crummy acoustics of the phone.

"It's Bill," the General responded reflexively.

"Okay, Bill," Orville said quickly. Without interruption, he continued. "Yesterday, during the meeting with the President, I got the feeling we were on the same page when it came to dealing with the problem we are facing."

"If you mean that the idea of armed confrontation scares the hell out of both of us, yes, we are on the same page."

"That's exactly what I mean, Bill. I think it would be a good idea for us to hash this out before Friday's meeting. Since the President told us to get out our thinking caps, I am going to infer that our talking this over in more detail is just what he had in mind."

"Don't expect any solid answers or great plans from me," said the General.

"Or me," said the Director. "But maybe when we put our heads together we can defy the odds and try to make two and two equal six."

"Where should we meet?" said the General.

After a pause, the Director said, "Maybe you should be asking where we *shouldn't* meet. In that case, I would have a ready answer: just about anywhere inside the Beltway; too many power lunches and too many tongues wagging."

"In that case, I have an idea. Do you play golf?"

"No," said the Director.

"Okay, you can basically say I don't either!" admitted the General. "I can't break a hundred with a bazooka." He said that as a light-hearted jest.

One of Bill Wieland's few regrets was breaking a wrist bone, the navicula, when he was a mediocre high school football player. He started high school when he was thirteen and three years later he was still on the reserve squad, the last player to be cut from the varsity. They divided the teams on the only day he missed football practice in four years. The reason he missed was to have a wisdom tooth pulled with nitrous oxide general anesthesia in his dentist's office. He was told by the dentist not to return to practice for at least three days, but wanting to avoid doing anything that would jeopardize his chances of making the varsity team, he went back the next day with his mouth still bleeding some. When young Bill asked the coach where he should report, he knew the squads had been divided the day he was out, the coach, "Beef" Matheson, said he would be playing with the reserves. "That is where we put guys who miss important practices." Bill was a standout on the reserves, but that was a hollow victory.

The accident happened in the second game of the season, against rival Denby High. Young Bill forced the runner to shift outside, sending him into the arms of another defender where he was tackled for no gain. During his abrupt shift to the outside, the runner planted his cleated shoe on Bill's extended left wrist and, in the process, turned the eight wrist bones into an abnormal nine. With an unusual, one-sided blood supply, this bone, when fractured, does not heal properly which left Bill with a life-long painful wrist that had no obvious deformity but limited movement apparent only to him. The essence of a golf swing for a right-handed player paradoxically depends on a strong left wrist. From that day on, any serious aspiration for golf, which young Bill was just getting the hang of, was gone.

Bill had an idea. "My adjutant was captain of the golf team at West Point and he has been given a special national membership at a new private golf club in Aldie, Virginia. It is not more than a forty-five-minute drive out in the country and we can have a nice private lunch there. Whoever said you had to play golf at a golf club? I am sure Adam can make the arrangements. Are you free for lunch tomorrow?"

"Absolutely. I am on."

The power lunch was set.

EIGHT

April 12, Wednesday

GENERAL WIELAND PULLED INTO THE CIRCULAR DRIVE at the entrance to the substantial brick clubhouse that looked more like an elegant home, a very large one. He drove himself so that one less person would know about this meeting. His usual driver was discreet, but why test him?

As he drove through the golf club property, he passed beautiful homes that he knew were each worth a million dollars or more. Quite a bit of vacant land remained, but there was lots of money in this town; it wouldn't be long before the entire property was built out. As he looked at the opulent spread, General Wieland thought about the choice he made when it came to his career. He was satisfied that being able to carry four stars on his shoulders made up for any deficiency in the hip pocket where he kept his wallet.

Actually, he was doing okay in the pay department, and he had security. As Chairman of the Joint Chiefs of Staff, with thirty-eight years of service and four-star ranking, his annual salary was $290,000. He had free healthcare, and it would only get better with the new rules allowing veterans to choose their own doctor. He had a car and driver when he wanted one. The best part of having a driver was that he never had to look for a parking place—a huge benefit in D.C.

He and his wife lived in Quarters Six in Generals Row at Fort Myer in Arlington, the official home of the Chairman of the Joint Chiefs of Staff since 1972. The 7,500-square foot home had a spectacular view of the Washington Monument from the third floor and was like nothing the General or his wife had ever experienced. Maybe a little over the top for their tastes, but they had to admit they enjoyed living there. With full Social Security, his income in retirement would not be a penny less than he was making on active duty. When you consider his pay equaled that of a Supreme Court Justice, he would not trade his stars for their robes or for the exclusivity of there being only nine of them compared to forty four-star generals currently on active duty. Another pleasant thing to contemplate was the likelihood of a good job; for example, working at a think tank and of earning speaking fees that he could expect based mostly on his experience in leading the successful surge in Iraq.

These musings were interrupted when he saw Orville McPherson pull up next to him under the portico. The Director had opted for his official car and a driver—his call. General Wieland stepped out of his car, handed the keys to the attendant, and waited for the Director. He mused how much had changed since the days of the birth of our country. George Washington had two hundred slaves and Thomas Jefferson was served by a young man he fathered with the slave Sally Hemming—and apparently did not even acknowledge him or give the bizarre occurrence a second thought. Orville McPherson was a man first, an African American incidentally, and an esteemed colleague who worked at the highest levels of government. Our country had come a long way. Bill Wieland was proud to serve next to a man like Orville and he only hoped the Director felt the same about him.

Entering the large lobby that continued the beauty and obvious care in planning from the outside, they spied ahead of them the dining room. The Grill Room could accommodate 115, according to a brochure Bill Wieland had read. Today it was set up for a much smaller lunch crowd. The General mentally calculated the sparse number currently dining compared to the number of personnel needed to serve them and he was glad he wasn't in the restaurant business. The maître de offered them a table by windows that were at least twelve feet tall overlooking the first tee of the golf course. At the edge of his view to the right were two immaculate, hard-surface tennis courts. They were blue. Bill Wieland preferred the traditional green. He had spent a lot of time on tennis courts. The only time he had to use his left hand at tennis was for the ball toss, and a stiff wrist was no handicap for that task. Tennis and boating made up just about all he did with sports—except for watching the NFL and the Michigan Wolverines on TV.

As the two men took their seats, both looked around. Their body language registered satisfaction with their selection of this place for the meeting. Nobody was within twenty feet of their table. When the waiter arrived, they placed their order: iced tea and the establishment's famed hamburger with a side of onion rings for the Director, and a cob salad and Diet Coke for the General. The two looked at each other across the table, waiting for the other to speak first. After what seemed like a long time, but was actually less than fifteen seconds, Orville McPherson spoke.

"Bill, I have the feeling we are definitely on the same page when it comes to the need to deal with that idiot in North Korea. When I spoke at Monday's meeting, I was thinking the best choice of action would be to get rid of Kim with as little fuss as possible. Even if we never touched him, some hackles would be raised and we would be blamed, but to be honest, in their heart of hearts, for those who have one, I think the whole world would be thanking us."

"You are right, Orville," said the General. "We could knock the crap out of North Korea with conventional arms if we could get away with it. We could employ pinpoint accuracy, creating almost no collateral damage. It could be clean and decisive. But that isn't going to happen. The Russians and Chinese would be pissing and moaning all the way to the bank. They would make the Sea of Japan look like a parking lot, and would be screaming nonstop with phony, righteous indignation. Based on all of this, I think we are in total agreement when it comes to the use of conventional force.

"When it comes to intervention with nuclear force, we suffer the handicap of being too civilized to strike preemptively. So, how do we stop the crazies from using the bomb when the world knows we will not use ours first? We have to ask ourselves if the next use of nuclear force will be a controlled, forceful deterrence or will it be in retaliation to whatever a rogue nation provokes with their own bomb? In the first case, there will likely be one event and, in the latter case, a minimum of two. But, there is no guarantee that a borderline country like Pakistan wouldn't use this as an excuse to use a bomb on another country, like India, and then all hell breaks loose."

The Director nodded. "I agree, there is no advantage in the use of force, conventional or nuclear."

"What in the hell do we do then, Orville?"

"We outsmart them by bringing together people in their

own country who are eager for a regime change," said the Director of National Intelligence.

"What assets do we have on the ground in North Korea?" asked the General.

"We have a handful of locals who are loyal to us. They can provide us with lots of information, but we doubt they can be effective when it comes to actually making things happen. They can tell us what's going on but they can't change what's going on. They do tell us that they believe there are several high-level people in the regime that are fed up with things as they are, but any action on their part, if they are caught, will mean instant retaliation—death. Kim's good at that.

"When it comes to inserting our own people, well, I don't have to tell you that there aren't any six-feet, blue-eyed blondes over there—and there are none who look like me. Dennis Rodman notwithstanding, black people don't exist north of the DMZ."

"That settles it for me, Orville. The ball is in your court."

"I know, Bill. I think it's time to talk with Bob Zinsky, the CIA Director, but it will be necessary to tread lightly."

———————

On the drive back to D.C., Bill Wieland's mind raced. He hoped they could find a way to solve a problem that was as imminent as it was seemingly unsolvable. He recalled his last conversation with Adam Grant and he felt that his aide had a good understanding of the situation but wasn't ready to share all of what he had on his mind. Adam wasn't all in when they had their last discussion on this subject. *Perhaps he didn't want to be presumptuous and that wasn't all bad,* thought the General. He would need to speak with Adam before the next meeting with the President.

NINE

April 13, Thursday

THE CHAIRMAN OF THE JOINT CHIEFS CAUGHT HIM-
self rearranging papers on his desk as he tried to
look more engaged than he really was. There were
other things he could do, but the most urgent was to come
up with a plan. He needed to do his part when it came to
providing the President sound advice. He was comfortable
with the policy decisions he made and the orders he gave
when it came to purely military decisions. He issued orders
based on his experience and knowledge of the situation,
with confidence they would be carried out by competent
subordinates. He had a good team and he trusted them, but
everything he looked at in front of him now seemed routine, unimportant—trivial compared to what was really on
his mind.

He and Orville McPherson, the Director of the National
Intelligence Agency, had agreed that each would do what

they could to devise a way to take North Korea to the woodshed over its saber rattling. They would come up with a feasible strategy and then develop suitable tactics—but right now, he was nowhere. At this point, General Wieland was coming up empty. He mentally looked at himself in a mirror. His all-too-familiar countenance said to him, "Bill, it's easy for you to describe a problem and then explain the options, but that is not why they put those four stars on your shoulder. It's your job to think of a plan of action that can be successful. Once you and the rest of the team decide what is best and the President signs off, that is when, and only when, you and your team know you've done your job."

Sometimes it was good to vent, thought the General. One thing he knew about himself was that he often was at his best when he was multi-tasking. Bill Wieland could attend a conference, and as the speaker droned on about something Bill either already knew or had no interest in learning, he could be busily writing. His jotting would have nothing to do with what was being said by the speaker. No. Bill, the thinker, would be pouring out ideas that were his own. These ideas were somehow unlocked by the masking effect of sounds and activity around him. An automatic blocking system clicked in and the words of the speaker actually cleared Bill's mind while enabling the outpouring of his own thoughts. Right now, with the North Korean problem on his plate, he needed an intellectual cleanse—not the GI kind, the brain kind. This was a concept he thought might have been uniquely his alone.

———————

Adam Grant looked up as his boss entered his office. It was a cozy, twelve-by-fifteen-feet with a desk, two file cabinets, and a small bookshelf that extended to just short of the ceiling. This two-foot space made room for mementos, like a baseball cap; photos of your folks; two leather statues of blue people from Morocco; and plaques of Jewish scholars, one old and one young; and whatever new thing you collected. All of these items could be shelved there, but none were. These were the types of artifacts that Adam had collected and liked having in his West Point dorm, but all of these memories were now ensconced in a storage unit, just a smidgen, added to the much larger cache of his parents who still lived in Indianapolis, but were downsizing. Since leaving West Point nearly eight years ago, Adam had been a nomad. No roots and no excess baggage. There was no window in his office, but an empty wooden window frame hung on the wall, a carry-over from the prior occupant. A small plaque that hung below had the message "Not a corner but a window."

Adam had traveled light ever since he left the Academy. He was comfortable with most of his belongings fitting into one hefty duffel. He was happy living this way. Half of him wondered if he should go back to school, and maybe he should, but the other half realized that between Afghanistan and his present job, hanging around with the movers and shakers and doing real stuff, he was learning a lot. While at West Point, he had spent three weekends in an abbreviated MBA course; he thought it was Mickey Mouse. Added to that, he just saw a review touting a book that said the Harvard Business School was the most serious enemy of U.S. capitalism that exists today. The book said the institution teaches that the sole responsibility of business leadership was to achieve higher stock prices. According to the author, business leaders feel they owe everything to their shareholders and nothing to society. This fellow was convinced companies routinely acted without regard to better the good of society. Adam didn't have time to read the book, but he was willing to accept the author's thesis based on the review and his own experience.

"Do you have a minute?" the General started.

"Of course, sir." That was the only acceptable response in this case, and it was sincere. Adam knew his boss had gone to suburban Maryland, driving himself, for a private meeting with DNI Orville McPherson. A limited membership to that golf club was Adam's biggest perk in his current position. He had time to take advantage of it only for an occasional round of golf and he had never eaten in the Grill Room where the General and Director had met. Adam only used the course about once a month, and he was glad for the opportunity to offer the services of the club to his boss.

"We enjoyed being there, Adam. Thanks for making it possible for a couple of plebeians to partake."

"My pleasure, General. When it comes to plebeians, the club has taken care of that by letting me in as a very junior golf member who can use the course for only a limited number of rounds and at off-peak times. I am sure your being there with the Director only added to the joint's class. Did they treat you well?"

"Yes, they did. And we had the room almost to ourselves. Confidentiality was our goal and we certainly achieved it. I must admit, though, just being there in the beautiful countryside was an end in itself; so much better than fighting the crowds that are always with us on the Hill. The lunch was great, but the subject was the pits. I am sure you know we talked about North Korea and their nuclear threats."

"Yes, I did," replied Adam. "Can I do anything?"

"Actually, you can," said the General. "My wife is in Chicago visiting our daughter, who works there for an executive re-location agency. Can you come over to our house tonight for dinner and a little private talk?"

"It will be my pleasure, General. Is there anything else I can do?" It was Thursday and Adam had no plans. Actually, he rarely had plans. He was a thirty-two-year-old single man who, but for the act of a terrorist, would be happily married to the love of his life. Adam was grateful for the all-encompassing job he now had.

"There is, Adam. But first, do you like Chinese food?"

"I do."

"Any favorites?"

"No. I like it all," Adam replied, and he did.

"Fine. Now, Major, here are your orders. Our favorite Chinese restaurant, Yen Ching, is just a few blocks from the Fort. I'll text the address of the restaurant to you. And I'll give you our address. I know you were there once, but just in case."

"Sure." Adam had been there at a reception the General and his wife had hosted shortly after Adam came onboard. He had only seen the formal first floor that was used mostly for entertaining. It was crowded that evening. Adam expected he would see something altogether different tonight.

"The food will be ordered for six thirty. You pick it up and I pay. Be sure to put in chopsticks, hot mustard, sweet yellow jelly, and soy sauce from the takeout tray. They leave it up to the customer to do that."

"Got it. I'll be there."

TEN

April 13, Thursday

Included in Adam's $1,975 monthly rent, which was covered by his housing allowance, was underground parking. The 665-square-foot apartment on Claredon Avenue in Arlington was only a mile from Fort Myer, where the General lived. From there, it was only another mile to the Pentagon, where they both worked. Either the 14th Street or the Arlington Bridge took them over the Potomac, which Adam sometimes thought of as a moat, and past the monuments to the heart of D.C. That was where the action was! He would drive to the restaurant in his own car, staying on the Arlington side, and then drive to the General's house. For unofficial activities and after hours, Adam wore civvies.

His small closet was not crowded. It held one pair of dark dress pants, a blue blazer, six neckties, and one dark-grey suit. There were also three pairs of khakis and an assortment of sport shirts. On the closet floor were four pairs of shoes suitable for four different levels of dress, ranging from military formality to utility—from smooth-toe black leather to canvas jogging shoes. Next in the closet were his summer and winter Class As, a blue dress uniform, and assorted fatigues. His one extravagance was to have his shirts professionally laundered and pressed, both military and non-military ones. A small dresser held his socks, underwear, handkerchiefs, sweaters, and other assorted apparel. His kitchen had only the bare essentials and his toiletries were typical Army: small in number, cheap, and useful. Tonight, he wore khakis, a long-sleeved plaid no-iron shirt from Costco, and cordovan penny loafers.

Adam drove up to the gate, showed his credentials, and told the military policeman the purpose for the visit. The sergeant examined his ID, turned, and entered a small guard house just big enough to accommodate him, and picked up a phone. Returning, visibly more impressed with the visitor now, the guard buzzed Adam through the gate. Adam was in his two-year-old Hyundai Sonata. He leased it for $241 a month, and this included military rate insurance. It was "plain Jane." MapQuest on his iPhone served his needs for assistance with navigation. The only add-on that was essential to Adam was the Sirius Radio connection. Adam had descended to a state of dependence when it came to Sirius. He couldn't have a car without it.

A car for Adam in D.C. was of marginal value. With the difficult parking conditions, Adam limited use of his car in the city mostly to those times when he was guaranteed point-to-point parking. The rest of the time he used a bike or walked, and Uber or Lyft. He was pretty sure the restaurant would have parking for carry-out customers. Most Chinese restaurants he knew of did half of their business with carry-out and this meant it was picked up by a customer in a car. These parking spots were like gold to the establishment, and because of stiff penalties for violations they were seldom abused. When he arrived at Yen Ching, he was happy to see that his luck was good today. He saw an empty spot that couldn't have looked any better if it had his name on it. He knew, once he was on the grounds of the Fort, he would be in a different and orderly world with no concerns about parking.

As Adam entered the grounds at Fort Myer, he took it all in with a clearer view than during his first visit, which was during winter and at night. He was struck by the combination of formality and uniformity. The place reeked of understated elegance, or maybe it should be called dignity. The homes were not elegant by usual standards, only by military standards. They were impressive because of the order, the impeccable landscaping, and the timeless aura. He imagined he could be visiting Omar Bradley or Maxwell Taylor a half a century earlier and it would look exactly the same. The officers' quarters to his right were duplexes. By their size it could not be any more obvious what the rank of the inhabitant was than if the insignia rank was displayed over the front door.

It was easy to find General's Row; the boss's directions were excellent. Once there, it was easy to find General Wieland's house. It was the same size as the larger duplexes in this section, but it was obvious from its single front door that it was not a duplex. He later learned that it had been remodeled as a single home in 1972 expressly for the head of the Joint Chiefs.

Adam approached the front door and rang the bell. The General greeted him at the door, looking more relaxed at home. He was fit and, even when he was attired informally, he exuded the aura of a soldier and a leader.

As they entered the spacious foyer, the General said, "Before going upstairs, let me show you around the first floor. The last time you were here it was too crowded for you to really see anything." Walking straight ahead, the General approached a long room with a large table at the center and said, "This is the dining room. It can seat up to sixteen for dinner. A large kitchen is next to it. When we have a 'to do' we hire a cook; that happens no more often than once a month, and that is the only time this kitchen is used." Pointing to the right he said, "This is the formal parlor, and on the opposite side is a smaller room for greeting people. If we have a big cocktail party, the entire first floor can be filled up, but thank goodness that is not often. There is an elevator over there, but let's take the stairs to where we really live."

At the head of the stairs, Adam saw a much homier atmosphere. The General said there were two more rooms on this floor; Adam assumed a master bedroom and a private study. The General ignored these and pointed out to Adam a large living room, parlor, smaller dining room, kitchen, and laundry. These quarters made Adam feel more at home. Downstairs was more institutional.

What looked like a newly renovated and thoroughly modern kitchen had a small adjoining breakfast area. The General motioned to the table and said, "You can put the food down on the table, Adam. What would you like to drink?"

"A Diet Coke would be good," said Adam, and then realizing he was too specific, he corrected himself. "Or a diet anything and, if not that, water is good."

"You don't drink?"

"Well, sir, no," he replied. And, as he had done probably way too often before, he offered an explanation that was totally unnecessary. "I gave it up for Lent four years ago and never started again. I learned in those forty days that you don't have to wake up with a headache just because you went to a party the night before." Adam could have explained further that his older brother and two maternal uncles were alcoholics and that he had drunk plenty of beer in his life but that he was much more comfortable now with his brain working full-time. There was no need to drag up the family or to cast aspersion on a lot of normal and successful people who used alcohol moderately, so he kept these feelings to himself. Adam did have to admit that he learned over the past few years that people drank a lot less than he had suspected when he was a drinker. He also came to realize that a cocktail party was probably the most boring place to be for the person who doesn't drink.

"Your choice, Adam. If you don't mind, I'll have a Scotch."

Why would I mind? thought Adam. He didn't reply.

As the General opened the carefully sealed bags from the restaurant, Adam saw a feast being spread. There were two egg rolls, two bowls of sweet and sour soup, pot stickers, and crab Rangoon for starters. For the main course, house beef and Kung Pow Chicken with steamed white rice completed just about a perfect Chinese banquet in Adam's opinion. They ate on plates, while serving themselves from cardboard containers, mostly in silence. Both used chopsticks expertly. Neither expressed interest in the barely sweet fortune cookies or the innocuous messages contained.

When dinner was over, the General said, "Now, my turn." He quickly returned all of the paper to the bags they came in and excused himself. "I love Chinese food but I hate the smell after I am done eating it. I am taking this stuff to the trash chute, I'll be right back."

Adam rinsed the plates in the sink, left them on the sideboard, and wiped down the table. Initially his mother and later the Army had taught him well.

Returning after disposing the trash, the General registered to himself approval of the small but thoughtful action on Adam's part. The General then began, essentially in mid-sentence, "What in the hell are we going to do about these bastards in North Korea?"

This was obviously a rhetorical question. Adam waited for the General to continue.

"Of course, you know that is what Orville McPherson and I talked about at lunch yesterday. We covered the same ground at the White House last week, and the group will meet again next week to continue its discussions."

"I know it is the hot button and, for what it's worth, I have been giving the situation a lot of thought," said Adam.

"That is what I expected. I would like to hear what you have to say. You know, in my job, I don't command troops. I only deal with the commanders who command troops at the pleasure of the Secretary of Defense, who gets his marching orders from the President. Outside of that, I simply give advice. If I can't share advice that is worth anything, I might as well give my pay back to the Government and just hang it up." The General's reply was in a voice more defiant than dejected.

After a long few seconds of silence, Adam knew he was on. "Well, General, I don't pretend to have any better answers than you, or even remotely as good, but here is what I think. A nuclear strike would get rid of the immediate problem but it would create new problems that we can only speculate about. One thing for sure is they won't be fun to deal with. Conventional weapons would only get North Koreans mad at first, and before we could disable their nuclear capability, I am afraid they could launch a strike. Besides, any prolonged build-up would get the Chinese and Russians on to us like a bear on honey.

"Trade sanctions, especially from China, and withholding cash will take more time than we have. Putting nuclear weapons back in South Korea and letting Japan have the bomb would also take time and could hasten irrational action by Kim. Regime change, after a spontaneous popular revolt, is simply not in the cards, at least not for now. Getting rid of Kim Il-un by other means would require decisive action on the part of people who are close to him but dissatisfied with his behavior. Can we find an effective group to do this? Does one exist? Is there anything we can do to help mobilize this spirit? Sorry, but I'm not much help, General."

"No. You nailed it, Adam. Using the facts available to all of us, you end at the same point as we did, and that includes the President himself, for that matter."

After a period of silence, while both men let the conundrum settle, Adam ventured, "General, it may be time to start thinking out of the box. Assuming the whole deal rests on Kim, and I think it does, do you think we can find a way to disable him? If we can't get locals to take him out, can we at least be there to encourage the best of the lot to step up when Kim is dealt with? What if Dennis Rodman had been one of our agents? He got close and personal with the Leader and could have dealt with Kim if he were so inclined. Too bad his visit was only for the purpose of creating notoriety for himself. The Leader seems to be attracted to celebrity—and that nutty basketball player seemed to fill the bill."

The General responded. "We already have assets in North Korea. They provide us with information, but they are not in the inner circle or remotely close to Kim. After this latest round of provocations, they have hinted that there is some discontent in the ranks in the highest echelons, but this needs to be confirmed and these people need to be contacted."

"So, what do we do?"

"I want you to work on this starting from where we leave off tonight. Keep this to yourself—I know with you it isn't necessary to say this—and remember whatever we do, there is a very definite possibility that we will need to employ the all-important PD. Let's continue this after the meeting with the President tomorrow."

Adam nodded. The General did not need to amplify or explain the code he was referring to. It was all too common behavior inside the Beltway: *Plausible Deniability*.

ELEVEN

April 13, Thursday

T HE PHONE IN THE PRESIDENT'S PRIVATE QUARTERS
rang. It was 9:34 PM. The President was in his small
office just off the bedroom. Incoming Presidents have
the opportunity to make minor changes in their private
quarters, and one of Phil Tripp's requests was to have a
conveniently located, small, and very private workspace.
This twelve-by-twelve-foot area adjoining the bedroom was
not much more than a large closet, but it fit the bill. It had a
desk and two computers; one was a desktop with the com-
puting elements on the back of the eighteen-inch screen,
with a separate, movable keyboard. This computer was not
connected to the Internet. The President used it to write—
compose. His handwriting was terrible. He recognized that
trying to put things on papers as fast as his thoughts came
resulted in his hand always being behind his brain. By the

time he looked at his handwritten material, or more realistically his hand-scrawled jumble, his notes were hopelessly unintelligible and that special moment of inspiration was gone.

On his left, a small return desk held a laptop computer that enabled connection to Google. This incredible service provided the President a wealth of information that never ceased to amaze him. Neither computer allowed Internet message traffic. The President was, in effect, in a cocoon, safe from electronic prying. All the back and forth in the White House was limited to official stations, especially those located in the Situation Room. For official business, especially signing official documents, Phil Tripp employed what used to be called a "beautiful hand." He had been introduced to this concept twenty years earlier when he met Arnold Palmer at a charity golf tournament. He heard the famed golfer say, "When someone does me the honor of asking for an autograph, it is my duty to make it legible." Phil Tripp could do this now, but when he did so, signing his name was the only thing he had on his mind.

A call on the President's private line from the Situation Room said that the call he had requested with the Chinese President would be connecting in five minutes. That would be 9:39 AM in Beijing, twelve hours ahead. This country, with a land mass nearly the size of the United States, only had one time zone. This policy was said to have been invoked by Mao Zedong in an attempt to create a sense of national unity. The President thought it made some funny times for sunrise and sunset, a problem that was dealt with in the United States by having four time zones.

The President made his way into the Oval Office to take the call, which would be monitored by a fully vetted White House Chinese translator. There would be no other officials on the line, but the call would be recorded, analyzed by the appropriate staff, and the President would share all of the pertinent information at the upcoming National Security Council meeting tomorrow. He was glad Secretary of State Pfister would be back from Russia and able to attend. As he stared at the phone, waiting to hear Xi Yun-ping's voice, the President wondered what Rutherford B. Hayes, the first President to have a phone in the White House in 1877, would think about a call like this. The President chuckled to himself. *Life is funny*, he thought. *I use the exact same desk as that earlier President, and it has remained the same, but the phone I am using is a heck of a lot different than Rutherford B. Hayes'.* For a fleeting second, Phil Tripp thought of the *United States Constitution*, which was like the Resolute desk: inviolate and solid. You didn't mess with it or make changes lightly. This current problem with North Korea was more like the phone: current and subject to updating and change. He then concluded there were things you have to preserve and others you need to deal with because they are always changing.

President Tripp heard the Chinese operator say in very good English, "Please hold for President Xi. He is approaching the phone now."

Knowing the President of the United States had the phone in his hand, Xi Yun-ping began. "Hello, Mr. President. I have been looking forward to this chance to speak with you."

"Thank you, Mr. President. And let me pass along to you and your family the First Lady's and my congratulations and best wishes on the birth of your first granddaughter." This was only a part of the international heads of state 'kabuki' that was routine in calls like this. It was like getting in the first blow to soften what could eventually end up in a knockdown drag-out contest; like combatants touching gloves before a boxing match. This was the kind of personal information, and there was usually much more, that was put in front of the President by his aides before every call like this.

"You are so kind, Mr. President. Our family is pleased with this new addition."

"I am sure you are, and for good reason," said President Tripp. China had only begun phasing out the one-child policy two years earlier, after it had been in effect for more than a half century. With certain exceptions, including in the case of some ethnic minorities, families whose first child was a male were expected to have only this child. If the first child was a girl, a family could have a second but if it were another girl they simply would have two girls. However, many believed that families whose first child was a girl simply got rid of the baby. The country experienced a dramatic decrease in the birthrate coinciding with this edict, but opinions are mixed as to whether this was due to the one-child policy or to dire economic conditions.

President Xi said, "I suspect I know the reason you are requesting this talk, Mr. President, but I will not be so presumptuous as to initiate the discussion. That is your prerogative."

"Thank you, Mr. President. I will get to the point. North Korea is making boasts and sending out threats that, if carried out, will have dire consequences for both of our countries."

"I understand, Mr. President, but North Korea is a sovereign nation. How do you propose that China act in a case like this?"

"May I introduce a hypothetical by saying you could act the way the United States would if Mexico were threatening China with a nuclear attack. We are close to Mexico and we are an active trading partner. But if they were behaving irresponsibly, in a way that promises grave harm, we would impose sanctions and apply whatever diplomatic pressure necessary to induce them to pursue a more peaceful course," said Tripp.

President Xi was quick to respond. "You raise a very interesting hypothetical but conditions in Southeast Asia are not as settled as they are in the Western hemisphere. With North Korea, we are dealing with a country that actually has nuclear bombs and a robust delivery system. We are totally opposed to arming South Korea and Japan, and we discourage any country, including yours, from engaging in war against North Korea with conventional weapons. We will continue our economic sanctions but can do nothing more. It is possible that working through the United Nations additional sanctions can be imposed. We will do nothing to oppose this, but as you know, Russia is likely to veto any move like this in the Security Council."

The conversation continued for another half hour even though the Chinese message was delivered in the first five minutes. The U.S. President heard it loud and clear: the Chinese would do nothing either for or overtly against the interests of the United States. They would go through the motions of continuing mild sanctions, and that would be it! The message the President would be sharing with the National Security Council was not going to be upbeat.

We are going to have to get into the weeds to deal with this issue, he thought after the call ended.

TWELVE

April 14, Friday

As the National Security Council team was settling around the table, President Tripp realized he didn't have a heck of a lot to say. The last meeting ended with everyone agreeing the U.S. was in a pickle, and nothing had happened since, as far as he knew, to change the picture. Would anyone have a good plan? That was the President's hope, but his expectations were realistic and he doubted much would come out of this meeting.

"Welcome, ladies and gentleman," he began. "Some of you know about my call with Xi Yun-ping last night, but at the risk of repeating myself, let me review what was said." When the President finished explaining there was no significant change in China's position, he said, "Now, does anybody have some good news?"

"I am not so sure it's good news," volunteered General Wieland, Chairman of the Joint Chiefs of Staff, "but Director

McPherson and I met to discuss the situation. We agree that a preemptive nuclear strike is not feasible nor is a conventional attack against North Korea. Arming South Korea and Japan with nukes will take too long and will raise hell with China, and probably a lot of other folks. Economic sanctions will be effective but they, too, will take months or even years to be effective. It's possible North Korea's threats are just that, threats, because not even a nut could justify a nuclear attack on the U.S. because of a belief we want to take over their country."

Bill Wieland paused and turned to Orville McPherson, who took the baton. "We believe," said the Director, "that for all their threats, North Korea is more bluff than blast. Our recommendation is that the U.S. maintains a strong defensive posture in the Sea of Japan. Along with this, we station additional missile interception capability in both South Korea and Japan, and the hell with what anyone says about it. We must remain on twenty-four-hour alert and intercept any missile that looks anything like it has the capability to reach even Japan. While this is going on, we re-double our efforts to infiltrate the North Korean leadership and, in the process, to inspire the North Koreans to dissuade their Leader by whatever means necessary, and replace Kim Il-un with more reasonable leadership led by people who can assume control and act responsibly. We propose that this strategy be given a three-month window to show progress and that all else done by us during that timeframe be watchful and defensive. And, I stress, *any intervention* will be internal, locally inspired, and carried out, and will take place solely in North Korea."

When he was finished, Orville McPherson looked around the table to appraise the group and look for any response. He saw faces that were intent and thoughtful but no one looked like they wanted to speak. This he took as a tacit acknowledgment that no one had anything better to offer. At the same time, there was no praise offered for this plan. Not surprising. Orville and Bill Wieland would have eagerly accepted a better idea from someone, but the silence confirmed it wasn't going to happen.

The President broke the ice and said, "Orville, where to from here?"

"I will speak with Bob Zinsky, the CIA Director, and get a full rundown on our operatives in both North and South Korea. From there, we will go mostly dark. With your concurrence, we will run a need-to-know operation for the duration of our three-month window. We will consider our remit is to stop a nuclear attack from North Korea on the United States. The tradeoff to accomplish this is effective covert action to thwart a nuclear warhead from reaching the United States. Need I say more?"

These were sobering words for the President and his advisors to hear. Did Tripp want to peel this onion further and hear details he didn't really want to know? He chose to say nothing and simply shook his head.

The meeting was adjourned.

THIRTEEN

April 15, Saturday

THE ALARM WENT OFF ON HIS iPHONE AT **6:00 AM,** BUT Adam was already half awake and planning his day. That is the way he liked to do it. Have a plan and make minor adjustments, if needed, along the way. Major Adam Grant liked to have a course of action and complete what he had set out to do. No getting off the hook or copouts. Even when it came to mildly unpleasant tasks, if they were part of the plan, in almost every case he would complete them. If he thought something should be done and circumstances didn't change significantly, he would do it. Dodging tasks just because they were inconvenient or not exactly what he wanted to do now was not the way he operated.

Of course, there could be exceptions. If his doctor canceled the MRI for a good reason, such as getting enough information from the CT scan, hooray! Adam got claustrophobic in what he called the "living coffin" of the MRI.

The first order of the day was a two-mile run on the grounds at Fort Myer, and continuing to the edge of Arlington Cemetery. Then he would shower and shave before going to his office at the Pentagon. His boss would be giving a briefing on Wednesday to a group of about fifty commanders to update them on North Korea, the issue that was commanding almost all of the attention around headquarters these days. General Wieland had asked Adam to prepare some handouts so that Trudy, the majordomo of the office support staff, could make sure they were duplicated, bound, and ready for the session.

Adam was a full generation younger than General William Wieland and much had changed in the area of communication in that relatively short time, about twenty years. His boss liked to share a particularly illustrative anecdote about this change ...

"Not long ago," Wieland said, "I asked a new clerk to find a carousel in the closet where the audiovisual equipment was stored. 'What's a carousel?' she asked. 'They are for projecting Kodak slides,' I told her. 'What's a Kodak slide?' she asked."

Adam knew Dorothy. She was a twenty-two-year-old civilian employee, a graduate of Butler University in Indianapolis, and a whiz at everything on the computer. Just last week she had, on her own, figured out how to add voice to a PowerPoint presentation using a program that could be purchased for a one-time cost of thirty dollars. She proudly asked Adam if he preferred the British voice of "Nigel" or the Midwestern tones of "Bill."

Adam placed his prowess with technology somewhere between the General and Dorothy, slightly closer to Dorothy, but never in competition. He liked designing projects and fully understood the concepts involved, but in no way could he compete with Dorothy, for whom all things computer were a virtual first language.

Adam and the General had discussed the importance of efficient communication. His boss was a good listener, let Adam talk, and was open to new ideas. Adam once shared his own concept of the difference between informing and teaching. If the General had already thought this through on his own he didn't let on. Adam's shared his idea enthusiastically: informing, he thought, was a relationship between independent entities. The convener would simply tell the audience what was on his mind, what he thought, and it was up to the people who heard to deal with it and use the information as they saw fit. This would often be in the form of speech that was written and read before the audience. That was okay for policy.

At the other end was teaching. When teaching, the speaker imparts knowledge for the audience to absorb and then use to carry out a specific task. The listeners should be able to do something after the teaching session, something that they couldn't have done before. Adam described the different purposes thusly: you share information to explain why it is important to stop your car before hitting something, and you teach how to apply the brakes to avoid hitting something. It turned out that on many occasions there was a bit of each in a given session, and that would be the case at Wednesday's meeting.

It was obvious the General knew exactly what he wanted to teach the group and also what he hoped each of the listeners would do with the information. Adam felt it was his job to assemble the material the General had outlined in his notes and put it in a PowerPoint presentation using mostly bullet points. Being able to see the points would help the General get his message across. This organizational style had worked the first time Adam had used it for the General.

Adam put together twenty PowerPoint slides. They

included the facts General Wieland would be imparting, and provided a framework for his presentation. He would be saying much more; the PowerPoint images would mostly serve to keep both the General and his audience on track. His talk would be unscripted and delivered in a relaxed manner, but it would also be packed with information necessary to bring the group up to date on Kim Il-un and the North Koreans; a conversation and not an oration. As a bonus, the PowerPoint material could be printed by Trudy's team to be used as a handout. Adam would be finished by noon. Then he would return home for more serious thought about the issue that was pervading: North Korea and the bomb.

Adam's apartment was the perfect size for his needs. The balcony was a generous eight-by-five-feet. It was a great place to sit, nine floors up, on a cool evening. Adam had lucked out when this prime location just happened to be available. From his balcony, he had a great view of the Washington Monument and the outdoor space would be a plus for any guests he might have who smoked, although he hadn't had one yet. In the living room, he had a sleeper-sofa, three chairs, and a fifty-five-inch VIZIO TV mounted on the wall opposite. Against the outside wall was a small desk with an all-in-one desktop computer with an eighteen-inch screen. Adam had a few books stacked on the floor, but only those that were essential. The rest were at his Pentagon office. When the need arose, he brought them home. Today, he didn't need any special reference material, at least nothing he couldn't find on Google. Today's job was mostly cerebral, to formulate a plan.

These were the parameters: the North Koreans had to be dealt with so that the country would be rendered incapable of threatening a nuclear attack on any country, but especially the U.S., which had been openly threatened on numerous occasions. As a start, China might be convinced to impose sanctions on North Korea to create an economic situation that would at least slow down North Korea's nuclear program. The problem when it came to counting on China was that North Korea was a convenient thorn in the side of the U.S. Because China was seeking hegemony in Southeast Asia, keeping America occupied by any means was in China's best interests, but this did not extend to nuclear conflict. South Korea and Japan might be set up with nuclear capability by the U.S. and thereby pose the threat of instant response to any bad action by North Korea. However, the strategy of having a nuclear surrogate on the other side of the world certainly didn't work for Russia when they tried to arm Cuba. Arming Japan and South Korea was out of the question. The U.S. could carry out a preemptive nuclear strike on North Korea to knock out their nuclear capability and inflict a great deal of damage to a country that was already hurting. Or, instead of nuclear force, the U.S. could employ conventional weapons.

Most countries recognized all of these options and the potential harm from a domino effect that could be unleashed. Each country would have its unique way of responding— but something bad could happen with any type of action. It was recognized by all that if North Korea attacked the U.S. or another country for that matter, there would be a ripple effect around the world that would affect millions. The world, in effect, would lose the innocence it had taken three quarters of a century to regain after Hiroshima.

Adam was convinced that if all of the responsible players on the world stage met in one room and a vote was taken for or against nuclear conflict, the vote would be one hundred percent against. But it was unlikely any country had a foolproof plan on how to avoid a nuclear conflict. Each country would, no doubt, have its own, understandably self-serving, approach. Secretary of State Roger Pfister's recent speech detailing the futility of nuclear conflict to the

UN was outstanding, but it was a watercolor wash. It set the stage but the finished product needed to be carefully crafted and, in the final analysis, it relied on the good intentions of all.

To Adam, the solution was getting rid of Kim or, at least, getting rid of his influence. It was impossible to be certain, but there seemed to be no other voice in North Korea except Kim's. Kim wielded the power and was clearly in charge. His influence on his countrymen could be compared to Louis XIV, the Sun King of France, who reigned for seventy-two years until 1715. Although it seemed Kim's power was nearly absolute, his "radiance" paled in comparison to the King's

Adam sat at his desk, staring at the computer screen. On the MSN home page was an image of James Bond Island in Thailand. It looked like a totem only bigger at the top, with scraggy trees sticking out. *Sitting here and staring at the computer isn't getting me anywhere*, thought Adam. *I'm done thinking about the options. It's time to do something before it's too late. Maybe I have to do something crazy, but what?*

FOURTEEN

April 15, Saturday

Adam jumped in the shower. It was getting late. Tonight was his bimonthly dinner date with Brenda. By mutual agreement, and only after she insisted, they would meet at their favorite restaurant; Smee's Grill and Bar, at six thirty. She did not want Adam to pick her up. Brenda set the parameters the first time they had dinner together. "We're not in high school and, after all, I am pregnant with another man's child. I am lucky to have you around under any circumstances. I can get to the restaurant on my own."

Brenda was a great gal and was expecting her and Chad's first child in September. He was serving in Afghanistan. Three months ago, he left the States for his second tour, a bummer with the baby coming. There was some hope Chad would be home for the big day. He was Adam's

West Point classmate and a good guy. His expertise was in communication, and he was re-deployed to get a few things straightened out with how the units were talking to each other. There had been some unfortunate interceptions by the Taliban and it had cost American lives. Knowing Chad, Adam was sure he would get the job done; and, with his first child expected soon, Chad would get the job accomplished as quickly as possible.

Adam arrived at Smee's via Uber at six fifteen. It was one thing to meet a lady at the restaurant, but it was a totally different thing, beyond the pale, to arrive late and make her wait. He stood out front. She would Uber also. It was a slightly cool evening and Adam was glad he was wearing a corduroy jacket. It was almost a sports coat, but he kept it in his hall closet like an outer coat. He couldn't get used to the new way of going to a restaurant in just a shirt, and some guys just wore a t-shirt. Adam was a little formal in this regard. It was a personal choice that made him feel better.

Right on the dot at six thirty Brenda Gale hopped out of the back of a grey Ford Fusion. The fare had been calculated and paid with a credit card in the final blocks and there was no tipping with this service. Brenda was a pretty girl. She was athletic, upbeat, and fun to be with as a friend. She was not showing yet, but she did have that unmistakable glow that said "Look at me! I am going to be a mother—and I want to do it right."

"Hi, Adam. Did I keep you waiting?" was her cheery greeting.

"I waited as long as anyone is expected to when the person they are meeting arrived on time," was Adam's rejoinder.

They headed into the restaurant. It wasn't necessary to make a reservation, the place was pretty informal, but it was a Saturday so Adam had called ahead. They were seated in a comfortable booth big enough for four.

"What do you hear from Chad?" began Adam.

With only the slightest hint of concern, Brenda replied, "About what you'd expect. It kills him to be away at a time like this, but he is a professional and he takes it like a man. I just hope he isn't worrying about me. I just tell him to keep his head down." Brenda continued after a short pause. "He really appreciates you looking after me, Adam. It means a lot. He did say he was jealous, but only in a good way."

Adam and Brenda had dined together twice a month since her husband went overseas. Adam was also on call for any emergencies that came up; so far there had only been one. Brenda had lost her car keys so Adam brought over a spare Chad had asked him to keep while he was gone. Before he had departed, Chad had said, "Here, Adam. Take this key. I hope you never need it, but I'll put my money on Brenda misplacing her keys at least once while I'm gone." He was right.

When the server approached, Brenda ordered iced tea, a dinner salad, and a salmon entrée. Adam ordered a Diet Pepsi (he knew Smee's only featured Pepsi products) and a French dip made with a delicious, sliced tenderloin with au jus, and whatever vegetable they were featuring. This was a Smee's specialty sandwich.

While they waited for their dinner, their conversation covered what Brenda was doing at her job at a high-end travel agency for the rich and famous. Adam skirted the issue of what he was working on. The problems Adam dealt with at work seemed like they were in the all or none category. If he couldn't share what was bothering him, he wouldn't say anything of consequence at all. His demeanor was circumspect and Brenda was sharp enough to know it must have been for a good reason.

With dinner finished, it was time for coffee and dessert. Both opted for Smee's famous Key lime pie. Brenda assured Adam that she was doing all she could to keep her weight gain in the acceptable range and that her only indulgence with dessert was with Adam because she knew he didn't like to eat dessert alone. She wanted to keep Adam happy because he was her favorite dinner partner, after Chad.

After the waiter re-filled their coffee cups, Brenda said, "Adam, I get the feeling you have something like half the weight of the world on your shoulders."

Chad is a lucky fellow, thought Adam. *She gets it*. The latest big news was that North Korea had succeeded in testing a truly intercontinental missile, which left little to doubt when it came to the U.S. being in trouble. The situation was definitely heating up and, to any thinking person, the pot was threatening to boil over.

"You are right, Brenda. Things are in a mess and, in this situation, I have to tell you that the public knows just about as much about what is going on as the brass and higher-ups know. It is all out there. The North Koreans have the bomb and a missile to deliver it. The only slight unknown is with the actual targeting and trigger mechanism. They may not have all of the details figured out yet, but they will, and it won't be long."

"What are we going to do?" said Brenda. In a thoughtful moment she said, "With a baby on the way, I have never felt more responsible for doing my part in keeping the world a place that is safe and healthy. Just a mom-to-be … am I nuts?"

"No, you're not. I feel the same way," said Adam. "I don't think I am telling tales out of school, but everyone in-the-know believes that we are embarking on the truly unknown. This is the first time in history that a nuclear power is overtly threatening another country that also has nuclear capability. What is going on today is far more serious than the posturing of the Cold War. The Russians were nasty fellas, but there weren't crazy. We are facing a bona fide threat from an unstable person capable of doing just about anything. If he isn't crazy, he certainly acts it."

Reading the seriousness in his voice, Brenda suspected she had touched a nerve. In turn, Adam realized he may have said more than he should have, or at least said it in a more definitive way than he should have.

Brenda decided to push a little further, not for her sake but because she thought Adam was about to burst. "Adam, if there is one thing I know about you, it's that you are a man of action. I can't believe you don't have this thing already figured out."

Alarmed by the prescient comment, Adam said, "Here is what I think. With all external action ruled out, it will be necessary to take this regime down from within. I am not sure how it will happen, but if we don't act, we are in for a bad time."

The atmosphere was getting a bit tense, so Brenda decided to lighten things up. "You know, there is really nothing new when it comes to human behavior. Maybe bombs can change what we do, but why we do things is pretty much hardwired in our DNA."

What is she saying? Adam thought.

"When you say that disarming the North Koreans would be an inside job, how about comparing what the Greeks did to the Trojans? They made something so tempting that the Trojans let their guard down, hauled the horse into the city, and unbeknownst to them, it was full of Greeks who were able to do enough mischief to make it possible for their army outside to come in and capture the city."

Adam looked at Brenda and could see she was tired. She had wrapped up a busy week and he knew that when any of their talk got serious, she started to worry about Chad. Adam wanted none of that. "Hey, good-looking, it's time to get you home and to bed. Remember, you are sleeping for two. Call me when you get settled. I'll get you into the Uber here, but I want to know when you are safely home."

This thoughtfulness made Brenda appreciate Adam for the great guy he was. Then a sad memory flooded her. Brenda knew that thoughts of Amy were not ever far from Adam's mind.

They went through the usual ritual of Brenda trying to pay, but this was another old-school habit for Adam. He paid. "It's okay, Brenda. Wait till you see how many times I have my feet under your dining room table when Chad gets home."

FIFTEEN

April 16, Sunday

ADAM DID NOT JOG ON SUNDAYS. INSTEAD HE WENT down to the weight room for an hour-long work-out, mostly with the machines. Then he had a quick shower, dressed, and made the half-mile drive to St. Agnes for 8:00 AM Mass. Adam hadn't been great about this lately, but today he felt he needed a talk with God, and where better than in His own house?

After church, Adam would spend the rest of the day trying to come up with a workable plan to deal with Kim Il-un. He had the sense General Wieland was counting on him for something of substance.

Later that afternoon, back in his apartment, Adam was thinking about Kim Il-un's attraction to celebrities and his affinity for the unusual and shocking. This could be what led Kim to have his picture taken with the Dennis Rodman.

There was no way a washed-up athlete, best known for his bizarre behavior, bleached dreadlocks, tattoos, and piercings could have gotten close to the Leader on other merits. Rodman was able to get close to the Leader because of Kim's weird attraction to notoriety. And, with not much else known about Kim's true personality and his life in general, maybe there was a way to capitalize on this proclivity; maybe this could be his weakness.

Adam started at the beginning to look at the problem by asking three questions: What can we do? What can't we do? What should we do? He started typing on the computer.

The problem: The unstable leader of North Korea, a country with nuclear bombs and a delivery system, is threatening to attack the United States. This threat is based on Kim Il-un's unfounded belief that the United States posed an imminent threat to his country.

A political/diplomatic response: The U.S. can work through the United Nations, relying on public opinion, applying pressure, and impose economic and trade sanctions and boycotts to force North Korea to abandon its nuclear threats and eventually disarm.

Threat: A display of nuclear or conventional force from the United States, and/or from South Korea and Japan; at the risk of incurring a monumental political response equivalent to a second cold war, only bigger.

Pre-emptive force: Destroy North Korea's nuclear capability with conventional warfare or with a pre-emptive nuclear strike. The former would be a logistical nightmare, spark a devastating attack on Seoul, risk provoking a wider conflict, and could be too late to stop a nuclear strike from North Korea. A preemptive strike of a nuclear bomb would very likely change the world as we know it.

Retaliation: The use of a nuclear response in the event of a preemptive strike by North Korea would be a disaster that begs the question "How did we let this happen?"

Regime change: Use any means possible to disable Kim Il-un and replace him with a more reasonable/stable leader. This could be accomplished by locals with whatever assistance was needed from covert U.S. assets.

Adam sat back and read the list on the computer screen; then printed out a hard copy for closer study. After several minutes of contemplation, Adam came to the unambiguous conclusion that the last solution was the best, actually nothing else even came close, and that a regime change should happen from within. There must be some world leaders who recognized the path of the current Leader was absolutely insane and dangerous. *How does a regime change come about? First, remove the leader and second, have a group ready to immediately move into power with as little disruption as possible.*

The U.S. knew that the seemingly intransigent Leader enjoyed the limelight and was attracted to celebrity. Kim was front and center at any celebratory event and, when it was to his advantage, he was sometimes accompanied by a person whose presence added to the occasion—but first and foremost it was always Kim.

Adam recalled the conversation he had last night with Brenda Gale over coffee and Key lime pie. She had told the story of the Trojan horse that was such an attractive temptation the Trojans let their guard down and opened the gate of their impregnable fort, which allowed the Greek army outside the walls to enter and conquer the compound that had withstood their assault for three years. This was a classic example of letting an attractive but un-vetted attraction get too close and ultimately take you down.

GENE HELVESTON

Adam was getting somewhere. Who would Kim rather have at his side when attacking the United States, than an important person of consequence? One with gravitas? What type of person would this be? For starters, the person should be relatively young. Someone like Henry Kissinger or a Supreme Court Justice would be too old and would not make as much of an impact on the young and impressionable North Koreans. The person should be young enough to attract the generation that was coming of age and should also relate to as wide a population as possible. Not to be a misogynist, Adam was not, but the world had already had Jane Fonda. She was only treated derisively when she posed on a North Vietnamese tank—it would be hard to get a female with more celebrity. The elimination process Adam was employing seemed to settle on a relevant male who was not too old.

What type of lifestyle should this male lead? Not an accountant, a cleric, or a professional. The person should have an aura of authority and be at a level that was universally recognized. The power of this person should be seen clearly. He should be admired and, above all, relevant. A scientist would be in too narrow a category and possibly kooky; a politician could be considered opportunistic and not trustworthy. How about a military man? Yes, that could be an ideal profile.

Adam stood, turned, and looked at the mirror on the opposite wall. He could hear the image say, "The guy you are talking about is me!" Adam's mind raced—in overdrive. It was one of those magical times when everything rattling around in his brain was virtually on fire with creativity. Then, it happened. Who better to be the Trojan horse than the person profiled in the spring issue of *West Point* magazine? He was a new West Point graduate whose father just became the first Korean to receive General rank in the United States Army. In addition, his grandfather was an officer in the South Korean Army during the Korean War. Adam didn't actually know this guy, but he knew a fellow with credentials almost identical to this guy.

John Yuen was his name. He had been a year behind Adam at the Academy. Adam didn't remember a lot about John but he could get all the information he needed online. When he Googled the West Point graduate page, Adam typed in John Yuen, and there he was. There was no information about grades or class standing, but Adam remembered the old adage: what do you call the guy at the bottom of his medical-school graduating class? Doctor! John Yuen was a nice-looking Korean of average height and in good shape. He had participated in intramural athletics, but his main extracurricular activity was the Glee Club. Adam knew this group had a demanding schedule, and to be eligible, members had to have good grades. He sounded like a good guy—a solid citizen.

The challenge was how to get a West Point graduate, who was a Captain on active duty, to publicly denounce his country and abandon his career, family, friends, and maybe his life, to head off a catastrophic event that could have worldwide consequences? Add to this the reality that this world-shattering event might or might not occur. Moreover, the proof of the need for this sacrifice would only be known for certain if the effort failed. Success, on the other hand, could be attributed preferably to a change of heart on the part of the Korean people. This could be a hard sell.

In the scheme that was racing through Adam's mind, the defector would travel to North Korea in civvies with a false identity for travel. His true identification as a Captain in the U.S Army would be revealed with as much publicity as possible after he arrived in North Korea. Upon his arrival in North Korea, the defector would make himself known to the authorities and express his admiration for Kim Il-un. He would loudly and convincingly declare that the U.S.

was evil, greedy, racist, and strove for world domination. He would expose the U.S. as not being as powerful as they led people to believe. If he had the chance, he would tell Kim there was no reason for Korea to be worried about an attack because political dissent was paralyzing the U.S. All Kim had to do was keep up the threats. In many ways, the threats were as good as or better than actually delivering a bomb. The defector would use these tactics only as a delay if necessary. The working hypothesis was that Kim would eventually carry out a preemptive strike. There was no certainty that he was content only making threats. The only variable was the timing of a missile launch—and before that happened, the necessary action must be taken to abort the strike by taking down Kim.

The only people to know the defector was a plant would be a select group in the Army and the CIA. Those in authority would convincingly denounce the defector because they would not be aware of the truth. This denunciation would hurt his family and his friends—but the wrath from the U.S. government and media would protect the defector because it would help convince the Leader that this U.S. defector could be used as a legitimate propaganda tool.

The duration of the assignment would be no longer than three months, and the defector would be in North Korea for no more than two weeks. While the defector was there, Kim would be replaced by a collection of sensible people who our assets identify as seeking better government and willing to act to make this happen. With help from the defector bringing down Kim, a change of leadership could occur immediately. An extraction process for the defector would be in place and ready for action at all times, in case it was ever thought the defector's life was in danger during his assignment.

The defector would be coached in his behavior, but it would be necessary for him to react as he saw fit as new situations arose. He would remain in communication with his support team, which would be located in Seoul and in the DMZ. The defector would be supplied with the most sophisticated communication devices available and he would be able to be in contact 24/7 with his support team.

A U.S.-based professional team with CIA backing would be sent to North Korea in advance to set the stage for the defector's visit. They would meet with and obtain necessary information from assets on the ground. Special attention would be paid to learning about and contacting known sympathetic government officials, military figures, and prominent citizens who could be recruited to support the takeover. Every effort would be made to only disable Kim keeping him alive but incarcerated. The plan would be for cooperative government officials to set up a provisional government and proceed with three main objectives: pacification with disarmament; a plan for re-unification with the South; and, when possible, free and fair elections.

The advance team would only be as large as absolutely necessary. Adam planned to volunteer to assist. His preference would be to lead or at least be a part of the small group that would go to Pyongyang in advance. Their task would be to meet with local assets and to arrange meetings with higher officials sympathetic to the cause and who could get close to Kim. Some of these might be North Korean diplomats who were already known to and who had developed relationships with their American counterparts; for example, while at the UN. When North Korea attacked South Korea they lost their seat at the UN. With the entrance of China into the UN in 1971, North Korea was granted observer status but has never sat on the Security Council.

Adam knew this advance team would be on a suicide mission if the wrong people in North Korea were alerted to their plan. The project had a lot of moving parts and each presented the possibility of introducing a weak link—but that was an unavoidable reality. It would be a house of cards that depended on the experience and judicious actions of people at several levels. In many ways, the preparation would be as dangerous as or even more so than the actual insertion of the defector because he would not be inserted until the advance team was sure that the framework for success was completed. The advance team would have to create a foundation on what could be considered the equivalent of quicksand. If the advance work failed, so would the mission.

When it came to the actual taking down of Kim, the defector would be at great risk, even with the most thorough preparations. Regardless of the outcome, his family would be subjected to the shame of their son and brother being considered a traitor—not good stuff. This negative consequence would continue as long as the assignment was active. If the plot failed, the defector would most likely be killed. He would be known as a hero-martyr only to the team. Eventually, President Tripp and other authorities would have to know the truth, but not while the project was underway.

With either success or failure, heads would roll, and there would always be doubters. If the plot worked, Kim would be deposed, the country pacified, and the world safer. The surviving defector would be a hero to the team, but would the U.S. Government be willing to reveal its complicity? Probably not. The ideal defector would be a highly qualified orphan with no family or friends who was willing to share success with a small and intimate group. Central casting could never fill that part.

Adam wondered who he should share his ideas with. He was fully aware of his marching orders from the General. "Give this some thought, Adam, but always keep in mind the people who must be protected by plausible deniability." It was this last comment that convinced Adam the General was totally serious. No fooling around with theoretical or philosophical aims. This was to be the groundwork for a game plan that had to result in a win. They were preparing for the Super Bowl of Super Bowls.

It would be essential to protect the President and those closest to him in the administration. They would be able to play their part in the scheme convincingly only if they were at least technically in the dark. Adam thought "technically" because someone as savvy as the President couldn't possibly think that the timing of events was simply a coincidence. As for the others, it would be decided who was complicit, who would be active, who would be able to feign ignorance, and who would be totally in the dark. Adam had some ideas, but the decision would not be his. The three highest in the food chain would be General Wieland, Director of National Intelligence Orville McPherson, and the CIA Director Bob Zinsky.

Adam was eager to meet with General Wieland in the morning. The keyboard seemed hot to the touch as he typed in words and sentences that seemed too preposterous to even record. The computer screen spoke to him: "Better if nobody sees this."

When he was finished, the material printed out at four pages. The word count was 1,156. If there was ever a need to duplicate this, it could be copied at the office. When the printing was completed, Adam closed the Word document and, almost reluctantly, selected "do not save."

SIXTEEN

April 17, Monday

ADAM WAS WIDE AWAKE AT **5:45 AM. HE HAD SLEPT** better than he had in a long time. His work yesterday was exhausting—mind-bending—but also purgative. Engaging in a purely intellectual process, using his brain with all-out effort to work through a complex, theoretical process was invigorating. Adam truly believed that a successful outcome from his efforts could have a profound effect, and whatever effort he gave the project his time was well spent. There was no way, even after all he had accomplished, that he had all of the answers, but he was pretty sure he had made a good start and he was sure he knew most of the questions.

As Adam began the short drive to the Pentagon, he decided to go over his main talking points for his meeting with the General. Talking to himself, he said, "Don't be wordy, but say enough, and be sure to stay on point.

No need to re-state the obvious by going over the seriousness of the current situation and the threat that our country
faces. Leave those things unsaid. And, above all, respect the
pervading need for plausible deniability."

Adam had been seated at his desk for no more than five
minutes when General Wieland arrived and poked his head
in the door. "I think we have a meeting scheduled," he said
breezily but unconvincingly. The General looked worried.

"Yes, sir. And I am ready," said Adam.

"Come into my office," said the General to Adam. He
looked at Cissy and said, "Please hold my calls, except for
you know who."

Typically, the General would have asked Cissy to bring
in a pot of coffee for Adam and he to share, but with his new
Keurig coffeemaker, a fresh, hot cup of coffee was available
any time he wished. It was one of the General's absolutely
favorite new gadgets. He began using one at home last year
and, in the process, he learned how important it was to use
distilled water to prevent scale buildup. He now used distilled water exclusively, and he had settled on Kirkland's
Pacific Bold for his stronger coffee and Starbuck's house
blend for a slightly milder brew.

The General's office was large. In addition to his impressive desk, he had two chairs and two comfortable settees
that faced each other with a low coffee table between, not
quite the Oval Office, but nice. The General sat in one settee
and motioned for Adam to take a seat opposite.

This would be a power talk, was Adam's take on how
the morning was starting.

"Have a nice weekend, Adam?" The General continued
the get-ready talk.

"Yes, sir. Do you remember me telling you about the
wife of a friend of mine who is in Afghanistan?"

"Yes. I remember you have been very nice to her, and to
your friend by extension. How is she?"

"She's fine and is expecting their first child in about five months. That will be about the time her husband, Chad, will be expected home."

"That's an awfully nice thing you are doing, Adam."

Before the General could say more Adam admitted, "Frankly, I enjoy Brenda's company. She's a great gal and doesn't have many friends, and in that department, neither do I."

The General knew about Adam's tragedy, but also knew it was time to get to the reason for their meeting. "I assume you gave our dilemma some thought over the weekend."

"Yes, sir," Adam responded. As he spoke, he started to open a document envelope he had brought into the meeting.

"No, Adam. Nothing on paper now. Let's just talk. Before we are done, you will know why I say this. What you have there, in your notes, I'm sure is important. I am not belittling your efforts, but for now, just our conversation will be best. So, tell me what you have."

"We both know the issues we face, so if it's all right with you, I will skip all the way down to the U.S. response option and what I believe is the best available course of action."

"Sounds good to me."

"For reasons that are generally agreed on, force, either nuclear or conventional, would be too dangerous. Political and economic sanctions would be too slow, and simply waiting for things to work out would be dereliction of duty. That leaves the option of regime change—cut the head off the dragon. In the case of North Korea, removal of Kim Il-un would be equivalent to cutting off the immortal head and putting an end to a dynasty. Anything less than removal of the immortal head would only anger the beast and a worse beast could grow back."

Impressive, thought the General, *he knows his Greek mythology.*

Adam continued. "When the warlike dragon is slain,

so to speak, there must be a peace-loving dove to replace him. It must be a big dove, powerful, wise, and with leadership qualities. The dove also must be on hand and ready to step in immediately. In truth, the dove should be part of the displacement process, so the transition moves ahead smoothly."

"Who is this dove?" asked the General. "Where is this dove? Is it willing and ready to provide better leadership and if it is so dissatisfied with the current Leader, why hasn't it done so already?"

"Good questions, General. Doves are peaceful by nature and are probably much more common than we suspect. The problem is they are known to submit to being locked up in a cage with only brief times out of it. It must take a lot to raise a dove's ire and, in a case like we are describing, a simple dove would probably require help to slay the dragon. To accomplish this goal, help could come from a bald eagle, and we know these are found only in North America."

General William Wieland silently pondered what he had just heard. This was the longest discussion he had ever had about a topic of importance without saying a word about what was really being discussed. It was clear to the General that his young adjutant knew exactly what he was talking about, and that he was both smart and well-read. The North Korean Leader must be taken down from within by loyal citizens who are within the circle of power, and who are both committed and potentially effective. The U.S. has no diplomatic relationship with North Korea, but with the United Nations Headquarters in New York there was the possibility of some interaction with North Korean diplomats in that setting. Beyond that, the only connection would be through agents in the country known only to the CIA.

"Adam, it is obvious you have thought this matter through thoroughly. I wish you had come up with a magic wand, but things don't work out that way, do they? From what you have told me, I think it's time you had a chat with DNI Orville McPherson. I expect after that, a meeting with Bob Zinsky over at Langley would be in order."

The General was relieved Adam had gotten his message from their earlier conversation about this. Nothing that was said this morning could be construed as his being in any way complicit. The General knew he should do everything he could to move along the project but he also had to distance himself so he could be useful another day. *This young man gets it*, the General thought. *I am glad he is onboard.*

SEVENTEEN

April 17, Monday

ADAM HAD JUST TURNED RIGHT ONTO WASHINGTON Boulevard. It was six thirty and he was heading home when his phone rang. With a bit of a struggle, he retrieved it out of his right trouser pocket and clicked on by the fifth ring.

"This is the office of Director Orville McPherson. Is this Major Adam Grant?"

Because Adam presumed it was a personal call, he had simply said hello instead of the formal, "Major Grant speaking."

"This is he," Adam responded.

"Thank you. Major Grant, this is Hilda Foster from the office of Director Orville McPherson. Please hold." There were lots of directors in Washington D.C., but inside the Beltway, the names of the higher-ups were so firmly coupled with the agency they directed that any further identification was unnecessary.

Adam quickly said, "Yes," but probably it was not heard, just inferred.

After being on hold for only a few seconds, a voice said, "Major Grant, this is Director McPherson."

Expecting his call, Adam said, "Thank you, sir. At your service."

"Major Grant, General Wieland told me he has kept you updated on the National Security Council's recent discussions. I am calling to speak with you about some possible solutions that have been mentioned, but which are now in a very preliminary state."

Director McPherson paused just long enough that Adam felt obliged to respond. Adam did not want to give the Director any inkling that he knew as much as he did, or had gone as far as he had with a possible plan. "I am willing to help in any way that I can," said Adam.

"Good. I thought you would. I have taken the liberty to contact the CIA Director and he has made time for us to meet tomorrow morning at Langley at nine. Are you available?"

"Of course, sir."

"I assume you know how to get there. When you present, out of uniform, at the main gate, the guards will be expecting you and will make arrangements for you to be escorted to Director Zinsky's office. I will be there also. Any questions?"

"No, sir. I will be there tomorrow at 9:00 AM."

Back in his apartment, Adam went straight to his computer. CIA Headquarters was located at 1000 Colonial Farm Drive in Langley, Virginia. Adam thought it was weird that, along with giving the street address and several pictures of the three-building complex, the CIA's website also stated: "We are an elite corps of men and women who conduct clandestine missions worldwide—collecting human intelligence that informs the president, senior policy makers, military and law enforcement. We are guided by core values for our professional and personal actions."

After a quick dinner of last night's pasta, Adam turned on Netflix and watched an episode of *Homeland*. It was almost surreal. The parallel universe of a fictional, but realistic, rendition of the nation's intelligence operations was unfolding in his living room on TV while he contemplated the real thing. *You couldn't make this up and sell it as fiction*, Adam thought. *Nobody would believe it.*

EIGHTEEN

April 18, Tuesday

A DAM WAS NOT TAKING ANY CHANCES ON BEING LATE
so he was on the road by eight. If anybody was
going to wait for the meeting to get started it would
be Adam. When Adam was attending West Point, his Uncle
Malcolm had given Adam a book called *The Silent Language*.
It described the many ways we communicate without
saying a word, and how powerful some of these messages
can be. Being late for an appointment was one such message to avoid.

Adam drove on Clarendon Drive to the George Washington Parkway, turned onto Dolly Madison Road, and
in four miles turned onto Colonial Farm Road. Along the
way, Adam had passed Saville Lane, where old friends
of his parents lived, Pat and Shelley Buchanan. Pat was a
famous author and TV personality who competed in the
1992 and 1996 Republican Presidential primaries and was

a presidential candidate for the Reformed Party in 2000. He had also written twelve books and was a founding member of three of America's foremost public affairs shows on TV, and was an advisor to three Presidents—a pretty famous man. Shelley was Adam's mom's roommate in the Theta House at the University of Michigan. Shelley had also held some high-level jobs in the White House. Nice people.

As he approached the gates of CIA headquarters, Adam realized the bucolic scenery belied the dark missions of the institution. Minutes later, Adam was sitting outside the office of the CIA Director Bob Zinsky. It was 8:50. After only a few minutes to collect his thoughts, Adam was called in, five minutes early. The large office had huge windows on one wall that overlooked a wooded scene. They contributed to the sense of peace and tranquility that seemed to be the paradoxical theme of the operation. The CIA Director sat in a trim leather chair next to the settee, where DNI Orville McPherson sat. Adam was beckoned to a seat similar to that of the CIA Director's. The three men were situated close to each other and, to Adam, this felt conspiratorial. When sharing secrets, it was natural to get close.

"Thank you for coming, Major Grant," Directory Zinsky began. "Director McPherson told me a lot of good things that General Wieland has to say about you. I have known Bill Wieland for twenty years and he is not given to dishing out bull, so you come well recommended."

"Thank you, sir. As I told Director McPherson, I am honored to be here and am at your service."

"Thanks, Major. But I am not going to hold you to that promise. When I tell you what we have in mind you may think differently and, if you do, we will not blame you."

"Sir, if I may. After two tours in Afghanistan, I think I have the will to comply with any reasonable request. The main reason I might be disqualified in this environment is lack of experience." *Was that too forward?* Adam wondered.

No, this was no time to mince words. What he meant to convey was that even though he was willing, he might not have the training and background to do what was required.

So far so good, was Bob Zinsky's feeling. *This guy looked the part of a heroic figure and he seemed to have the right combination of confidence and humility.* "Getting down to it, Major, this is what the General implied—without saying it in so many words ..."

Implied. Here comes that plausible deniability thing again. Adam almost winced.

"... with direct military force too risky and political and economic actions too slow, there needs to be a way to dissuade Kim Il-un from launching a nuclear attack. Our conclusion is that this should be accomplished by applying pressure from within. Frankly, based on the latest intel, the chances of Kim going nuclear are in the ten to twenty percent range. Of course, when it comes to nuclear attacks, any odds are too great to risk. As you know, our job here at the CIA is to collect actionable intelligence, and I stress the word *actionable*. The information we gather is the kind that is so important and at times so threatening that it demands something be done. 'Joe has a gun' is information. 'Joe has a loaded gun pointed at your head' is *actionable* information."

Orville McPherson chimed in. "I can only second what the Director is saying. The gun is indeed pointed at our head—and it is a big one."

McPherson was Zinsky's boss. It was clear to Adam that they were not only in concurrence, but they were acting with a sense of urgency.

"If we are all in agreement," Bob Zinsky continued, "the next step is to meet with the directorate."

In agreement on exactly what? Adam thought.

"Major Grant, I don't want to jump the gun, but I assume since General Wieland has been discussing this with Director McPherson, he will be willing to have you shift your activities over to us, on loan for the duration of the project, and during that time we will be getting to know each other better. Is that your understanding?" said the CIA Director.

"Sir, at this time I have no understanding with General Wieland with regard to the issue we are discussing. Perhaps Director McPherson can fill us in?"

Continuing the formality of the meeting and adhering to protocol, Director McPherson offered, "I have not discussed re-assignment of the Major in specific terms with General Wieland. But Bob, I think your assumption is correct." Turning to Adam, he said, "Major Grant, we will discuss this with General Wieland and we can proceed from there."

The meeting ended in forty-five minutes. The CIA Director told Adam he would be in touch with him tomorrow to discuss any further plans, and he thanked Adam and the Director of National Intelligence for coming.

It had been all business, not even an offer of coffee. Adam had the feeling that Orville McPherson was, in effect, removing himself from any active role in the project. He wanted it accomplished but he didn't want to know about it—plausible deniability.

———————

Adam made the short drive from Langley to the Pentagon. General Wieland was in Philadelphia today, and tomorrow afternoon he would be conducting the high-level meeting that Adam had been helping him prepare for. Taking a look at the attendance roster, there would be enough stars in that room to sink a battleship. Tomorrow morning's schedule would allow plenty of time for Adam to discuss today's events with the General before his meeting. *Who am I kidding?* Adam was sure the General knew more about today's meeting than he did. There was no doubt the General and McPherson had talked and had plans of their own.

When Adam arrived at his office he had a message to call Betsy Aldrich, Director Zinsky's Special Assistant. He called and was told that he should return to Langley at eleven tomorrow morning. She told Adam he should go to the lobby of the old building, not the new Bush building he was at today. Agent Erin O'Leary would meet him there for an orientation session. He should be wearing civilian clothes.

Adam was sure his meeting with General Wieland would just be to tell him that the plan had already been set.

NINETEEN

April 19, Wednesday

ADAM WAS AT HIS DESK AT THE PENTAGON AT **8:00** AM. He expected to see the General any minute. On the drive in this morning, he heard that Kim Il-un was claiming the CIA had made an unsuccessful attempt on his life a month earlier. Kim said it occurred at a huge military demonstration, but Adam couldn't remember what it had been called. Adam did remember seeing huge North Korean trucks on TV not that long ago pulling even bigger trailers stacked with fat bombs, which many people thought were empty and just for show. The parade was interspersed with goose-stepping soldiers and a host of other warlike paraphernalia. Adam felt soldiers goose-stepping was synonymous with bad guys. It seemed only dictators ordered their troops to behave this way. It was a miserable experience to move like that and nobody would do it unless it was demanded. The origin of this practice was obscure, but the explanation that made sense to Adam was that marching in this exaggerated way was designed to create a sense of unity with the soldiers and confidence in the population they were to guard. But, was it to guard and protect or was it the threat of attack that was the message?

Something was wrong with this new claim by Kim. First, there was no evidence of any disruption during the event, which was widely covered by the North Korean media for export. Kim's presence in the reviewing stands and description of his other activities were no different than Western viewers could expect. Why wasn't anything said about it at the time? If Kim just wanted to make a fuss, what better time than now as a cover for his threats? Secondly, Kim killed people who displeased or threatened him, or he sent them to labor camps. A plot hatched by the CIA would certainly be cause for a prompt and intense reaction, presumably with lots of heads rolling. Adam believed this recent accusation was just fictitious and presented as an invented excuse for something Kim intended to do.

The meeting in General Wieland's office at 9:00 AM was brief. The Chairman told Adam he would be re-assigned to Langley on a temporary basis, with a projected duration of three months. Adam's purpose at the CIA Headquarters would be liaison work, and the time frame would not be hard-and-fast but flexible. After the assignment ended, Adam would resume his duties at the Pentagon.

The General was brief and to the point. "You're coming back, Adam. I'm not letting them keep you. There will be no announcement beyond that you were reassigned. If people surmise it is for you to attend briefings and orientation sessions that would be just fine. You will simply be learning more about what goes on at Langley to assist you in your job here. It will not be necessary for you to keep me apprised of your progress. Orville McPherson and Bob Zinsky will pass along what I need to know. No need to pack anything from your desk. Leave it all here for when you return. I will have an aide on loan in the interim."

Adam wanted to say something, but what? The General was serious, composed, and focused. If he had heard the latest news about Kim he didn't let on, but it was inconceivable that he hadn't. "Thank you, sir," was all he said. Adam was sure that was all he needed to say.

The General closed with, "I know you have another meeting later this morning at CIA Headquarters. Good luck."

Adam went to his desk and opened the top drawer. He took out a miniature Swiss Army knife that measured only two inches and had seven blades, plus scissors, tweezers, and a ballpoint pen. The knife had survived West Point, two tours in Afghanistan, and had, for Adam, assumed the role of talisman. Adam could hardly count the number of larger Swiss Army knives he had lost or given up at TSA checkpoints, but this little one had stuck with him. Next, he took a smooth 1963 Lincoln head penny that he had picked up from the Walgreens parking lot this morning. It was lying on the pavement just outside his driver's door when he returned to his car after buying two bags of Lindor milk chocolates, one for Cissy and one for Trudy. The penny had not been there when he went into the store. Adam had seen nobody leave or enter the store during the brief time he was in it. He put the penny in his wallet behind his medical insurance cards, the least-used section and the safest place he could think of on his person. Pennies that mysteriously appeared at crucial times had become spiritual experiences for Adam; he had dozens of them. They were encouraging signs and today's penny was a welcome omen. Someone was looking out for him, and he was pretty sure he knew who it was.

As instructed, Adam was in the lobby of the old CIA building a few minutes before eleven. He had checked Google to find what else he could learn about Langley. His perusal found descriptions of the physical characteristics and history, although no other details about the cloak-and-dagger stuff going on now. He knew the concept came out of the Office of Strategic Services of World War II, and grew during the Cold War era. General "Wild Bill" Donovan was the first OSS Director and Allen Dulles came up with the concept of a college-like campus cloistered but close to the Capital; it was only eight miles away. The building Dulles envisioned and Adam was in now, contained over one million square feet and was nestled on a 238-acre campus surrounded by forest. It felt like a park. It was a place of contrasts.

On the other side of the Great Seal at the center of the lobby, a tall, dark-haired woman stood. On the grading scale, Adam couldn't think of a reason why she wouldn't rate a ten, but because he thought everyone should be given the chance to improve, he gave her a 9.5. In addition, the rating was always re-done after meeting a person and getting to know them better—for example, Brenda. He should call her for dinner later this week. He would have to find a way of explaining why he would be AWOL and unavailable for dinner for a while. In Adam's opinion, Brenda was a ten. She was good-looking, had a sweet disposition, and a brain as sharp as anybody he knew.

The young woman across the lobby, the only person he saw who didn't seem to be walking somewhere on a mission, was just looking straight ahead but not in Adam's direction. She had a look that to Adam's appraising eye was special. He didn't know exactly what to call it—comely or maybe classic? The word cute certainly didn't apply. Beautiful, yes. She looked like she could have posed for the Venus DiMilo statue but she had too many clothes on for that. No luck, today, though as he would be meeting Erin O'Leary, and she was definitely not this person he was admiring.

Before he got further in his musings, the woman started to walk toward him. As she approached, she questioned, "Adam Grant?"

"Why, yes." Adam almost stuttered.

"You were expecting to meet a red-haired, freckle-faced colleen." It was more of a statement than a question.

Although Adam conceded to himself that she had just read his mind, he lied "Not so. This whole deal is so new to me, I try to avoid pre-conceived notions or stereotypes." *Not a bad rejoinder*, he thought. Not really on the offensive, but at least he was staying even.

"Don't worry," she said. "I get that reaction a lot and I am used to it. First time here?"

"Well, almost. It's the second. I was here briefly yesterday."

"My job is to show you around Langley and to answer any questions you have about what we do, why we do it, and in so far as I can, how we do it. As you might expect, I know a lot about you because Director Zinsky provided me with your dossier. I realize that puts you at a disadvantage because you don't know anything about me. But don't worry, we will take care of that. And, I hope I can learn something about you that didn't make it into your bio."

The tour started. An impressive no-nonsense statue of Major General William J. Donovan had a bronze plaque that said he was the "Father of Modern American Intelligence Gathering." *If there was anyone you wanted to be in charge of stuff like this, it would be a guy who looked like that*, Adam thought.

Again reading his mind, Erin said, "Kind of inspires you, looking at him." Adam could only nod his head in agreement.

During the tour, Erin showed Adam the Fallen Agent Memorial, the Directors Portrait Gallery, the CIA Museum, the Library, the Melzac Art Collection, and highlights of the new Bush building. The Atrium Sculpture Hall featured the specialty D-Drone and other spy planes, including several versions of the U2.

Trying to figure out the psychology of the building and its setting, including its comprehensive and selectively guarded system for acknowledging those who contributed, and the sense of order that pervaded, Adam concluded he was immersed in a gigantic metaphor. The people who worked here seemed to actively or reflexively embrace the essence of the enterprise. They seemed to be a dedicated, orderly, selfless, enterprising, and fiercely loyal—a team.

After two hours, Erin had provided Adam a good representation of the highlights. It would take a week to see them all. For his part, Adam had seen enough and wanted to get into something substantive. He wanted to know more about what spies really did and he wanted to know how Erin ended up working here. He was delighted when Erin said, "How about lunch?"

"Yes, Erin. That would be great!"

"You have probably had enough of the CIA stuff. Are you up for Starbucks?"

"Yes, but ..."

"We have one right here on campus," Erin explained as she led Adam down yet another corridor. When they entered the café, she proudly announced, "Welcome to what we call 'Stealthy Starbucks'."

"I'll be darned. You do have everything."

"Before you get too comfortable, word has it that the chief of the team that got Bin Laden recruited a deputy over a latte in this place. Impressed?"

"Yes." Then he added, "There you go, Erin, raising the bar every time we round another corner!"

Erin told Adam to grab a table while she went to the counter and ordered a turkey sandwich and black coffee for Adam and a small green salad and latte for herself. They were both starved and the food was almost inhaled. Another reason for eating fast, though, was that both had a lot more to say than how impressed they were with the building and its storied history.

Without prompting, Erin started to share about herself. "I graduated from Florida State University, just above the Redneck Riviera, in 2012. My mom is half Korean and an ophthalmologist at Bascom Palmer Eye Institute in Miami and my dad is a cardiologist at Jackson Memorial Hospital. He is one hundred percent Irish. They met when both were in training at Johns Hopkins. I was born there, and am an only child. I didn't aspire to a career in medicine, and my folks didn't push me. For some crazy reason, I had a bee in my bonnet for the CIA. It started during my freshman year of college. I had a feeling I would need something extra to make the grade so I decided to learn a second language. I chose Korean.

"My grandparents live in a retirement community, The Villages, near Orlando. My grandmother is Korean and my grandfather is a retired one-star. They met in Korea, during the war. Between Grandmother, some college courses, and living six months in Seoul after graduation, I got pretty good at the language. Actually, I have had to fight off requests to be a full-time interpreter.

"As soon as I returned from South Korea, I applied for and was accepted to work at the CIA. I work in Operations. We call it the Directorate of Operations and our work is clandestine. 'We spot assets, then develop, recruit, and handle non-U.S. citizens having access to foreign intelligence vital to U.S. foreign policy and national security decision-makers.' If that last sounded stilted it is verbatim from the handbook. We are spies and we work with spies.

If there is anything more you want to know about me, just ask and I will answer if I can. If there is anything not in the dossier I have on you that would help me know more about you, I would like to hear it."

Adam was convinced Erin had it all together. "Do you know why I was summoned to Langley yesterday?"

"No." Erin was almost truthful.

"Do you know why you were assigned to give me a tour that could have been given by a docent and buy me a turkey sandwich that I could have purchased myself?"

"Yes. Because I have been here long enough to know what it takes to function in this environment, I was asked to meet with you and do my best to figure out if you had what it takes to tackle a job at a place like this. You could call me a preliminary human resources person."

"Is this your usual activity?"

"No."

"Was a person from Operations chosen for this preliminary interview for a reason?"

"I don't know, and that's the truth. I don't want to speculate and have to retract it later. The best I can do is say I have an idea, but speculation now would not be appropriate. I can tell you with confidence that we will both know what this is all about sooner rather than later."

After a thoughtful pause, where it was obvious Adam was trying to settle on just what to say next to the impassive but beautiful face across the table, he said, "Thank you, Erin. I guess that finishes us here."

"Yes, Major Grant. I would usually be calling the end to a session like this, but you are right. It was a pleasure meeting you and sharing some of the features of this very special place. I hope I'll be seeing you again."

"I didn't mean to be jumping the gun but things are in a bit of turmoil for me just now. I have been relieved of my duties at the Pentagon for three months, met with the

Director of National Intelligence and the Director of the Central Intelligence Agency yesterday, and I don't know what the hell is going on!" Adam blurted, before reflexively adding, "I hope I see you again too." He meant it.

TWENTY

April 23, Sunday

IT WAS EARLY. ADAM PUT THE DOUBLE-CUPPED TWELVE-ounce Dixie cup under the dispenser on the Keurig. He was looking forward to his first sip. He didn't feel wasteful about using two cups because he rinsed them and used the same duo throughout the day. This way the cup felt more substantial, and he liked that.

He would be leaving his apartment in about an hour to make the two-and-a-half-hour drive to Williamsburg. Adam had never been there. He had read accounts of George Washington, Thomas Jefferson, James Madison, and others who sowed the seeds for the founding of our country in that city. While the first shots of the War for Independence were fired in Massachusetts; the Declaration of Independence was signed in Philadelphia; and the first seat of Government with George Washington as President was in New York City; no city was more instrumental in the founding of our country than Williamsburg, where Patrick Henry uttered, "Give me liberty or give me death."

Director Zinsky's office had called Adam on Thursday morning at nine, following his pleasant tour of CIA Headquarters with Erin. When the call came, Adam was in his apartment. He had finished a good run, eaten a breakfast of shredded wheat squares (the small ones), almond milk, and fresh raspberries; and was reading the *Washington Post*, which took extra time to translate. The so-called straight news, if he could find any, had to be put into plain information in his mind with care. Flagrant editorial bias, he concluded, was present throughout the paper, not just on the editorial pages.

The call, not unexpectedly, was once again from Betsy Aldrich, Special Assistant to Director Zinsky. "Good Morning, Major Grant," she began. "I have a message for you from Director Zinsky. He would like you to report to Camp Peary this coming Monday, April 24th at 8:00 AM. Simply present yourself at the front gate, they will be expecting you. It is the plan for you to be at the Camp for five days …" She paused. "If all goes well. After that, you will be given further instructions. If you need to contact our office at any time, do so at this number." She gave Adam the number of her personal line. "The Director wants me to pass along his appreciation for you agreeing to begin this training, and he wants to make it perfectly clear that you understand that this training is entirely voluntary on your part. You have no obligation to proceed with the program if you don't wish to do so. Do you have any questions?"

"What should I pack for this assignment?"

"Wear and pack civilian clothes that you would wear on a fishing trip or a hike on the Appalachian Trail. Bring comfortable shoes, and include a pair of boots if you have them. If that is not convenient, you will be provided with a pair. You might also want to bring some running shoes.

Anything else you need in the way of apparel will be provided. If you take any special medicines, bring them along. If you wear glasses, bring an extra pair if you have them. No need for toiletries or shaving gear as that will be provided. You are not going to a five-star hotel, but Camp Peary is well-equipped."

"Thank you, Ms. Aldrich. This is very complete and I understand." After a brief pause, Adam added, "Should I be saying where I am going in case someone wants to contact me?"

"That is probably not a good idea. Where you are going is not a secret, but it is not something that you want to broadcast either. You will have your cell phone with you and you can receive calls and make outgoing calls as needed."

"Thank you, Ms. Aldrich. You have been very helpful. I look forward to meeting you one of these days."

"My pleasure, Major. Have a good day."

Of course, Adam knew that Camp Peary was the official name of a special facility that was built in 1942. It was essentially a spy school that, in the parlance of the CIA, was referred to as The Farm. At the outset of World War II a 9,000-acre tract was set aside for a military facility in York County on the Virginia Peninsula. In the process, several settlements were relocated, including the towns of Magruder and Bilger's Mill. Magruder was an African-American community established for freedmen after the Civil War. Adam considered the move as eminent domain on steroids, but the people were well treated and were moved together into a nice, new town only a few miles away.

The initial use of Camp Peary was as the Naval Construction Training Center where Seabee's were prepared for the important work they would be doing. This storied outfit was mostly responsible for building and repairing airfields on strategic islands in the Pacific theater in World War II. After that, the camp was used as a special prisoner-of-war facility. The prisoners interred there were mostly German submariners thought by their navy to be dead—lost at sea. The fact that these seamen survived was kept secret to ensure that the German authorities would believe that the secret-code books and Enigma Machines from their vessels were lost at sea and could not have been compromised. Knowledge that these had been recovered would have led to the Germans changing codes that had already been broken by Allied decryption. It was said that many of these German prisoners remained in the U.S. after the war and became naturalized citizens.

After a period of various civilian and military uses, Camp Peary morphed into its current status as The Farm. The Central Intelligence Agency used it for training its clandestine personnel as well as people from other organizations in the Government. The Camp was secure and accessible only to those specifically assigned to the facility. Any visitors were escorted at all times by military personnel.

The Sunday morning drive on I-95 and then on I-64 was pleasant. Adam planned to make a reservation at the Williamsburg Inn. Ordinarily Adam would have opted for a chain motel on the edge of town, but since he would have a whole afternoon to roam around town, he wanted to be within walking distance of the historic sites he intended to visit. However, when he discovered the price for a single room at the Williamsburg Inn was $455 plus taxes, he changed his mind. Back to the usual. He would stay at the Holiday Inn for $95 plus tax. Not forsaking all, he would have dinner at the Williamsburg Inn Rockefeller Room. That would be an affordable compromise.

The Rockefeller Room turned out to be a pleasant experience; an authentic continuation of the colonial atmosphere he had enjoyed for most of the day. Adam had Oysters Abby for a starter; then Braised Lamb Shank, mashed potatoes, and a zucchini dish he couldn't figure out for his main entree. For dessert he had melting chocolate cake that was ambrosia. The dinner service was professional and not provided by actors. Thinking about his afternoon of touring, Adam decided he was annoyed by the actors inserted at the historic sites. They went through the motions of portraying activities as they would have taken place in colonial times while carrying on banter in character for the benefit of visitors. Adam wondered if maybe he was too serious. Would it be better for him to be less critical; just go with the flow? Regardless, he knew tomorrow would be something else— the real thing.

TWENTY-ONE

April 24, Monday

L EAVING WILLIAMSBURG, ADAM HEADED EAST TOWARD I-64 and then drove twenty miles south to Exit 238. Veering off to the right, he looped around to State Road 143 and wound his way over the interstate to an elaborate access complex flanked by stout fencing. On the right, he saw a substantial blue-roofed building that looked like it was where he wanted to go. On the left, was a large turnaround suggesting it was common for cars to arrive at this point only to be summarily turned away. From the size of the pavement, it appeared that many more people were turned away than admitted, and by a wide margin.

Adam was greeted politely and officially at the gate by an enlisted man in uniform and identified himself. "Yes, sir, Major. You are expected. Sergeant James will escort you to your destination." The guard pointed to the only car in sight except for Adam's. "You can follow that car. After a quarter mile, you will turn right, and in a mile, you will be there. Have a nice day, sir."

Several things were immediately clear to Adam. They didn't let anyone in who wasn't invited. And even with simple and easy-to-follow directions, he would be escorted which meant even people who were supposed to be here were not allowed to roam the camp on their own.

When he arrived at the entrance to a parking lot serving a tight cluster of buildings, his escort stopped before Adam could turn in. Sergeant James approached Adam's car on foot. Adam's window was already rolled down. Sergeant James pointed to a T-shaped building, a little larger than the others, at the end of the parking lot. "You can check in at Building Three. They are expecting you. Have a nice day."

Sergeant James pulled his car ahead and Adam turned right into the large parking lot that looked like it could accommodate fifty cars. Adam noticed that Sergeant James had backed up and followed him into the parking lot, and remained there until Adam entered the building.

A man looking closer to seventy than sixty, with an indifferent shock of scraggly white hair that he apparently felt no need to rearrange, greeted Adam. He had probably been six one or taller a few years ago, but he was shorter now and slightly bent. He was living evidence we all compact a bit with time; an unwelcome "birthday present" that was better than dying. The man had craggy features that made Adam think of a burl in hardwood, deformed by time, wear, and inclination; handsome in its own way, hard, and valuable. The man presented as rock hard and looked like he could take care of himself, come what may.

"Welcome, Major Grant. I've been looking forward to meeting you." The voice coming out of the burl matched the rest of the picture. "My name is Amos Griggs. I will be looking after you for the next few days."

"I am looking forward to that, Mr. Griggs."

"Colonel, but Amos will do."

"Okay, Amos," said Adam. "And it's Adam for me."

"Good. Let's start by stowing your gear. I hope they told you that you wouldn't have to bring much."

"They did, Amos, and I did my best to comply. I usually travel pretty light anyway."

Adam retreated to his car and retrieved his regulation duffel that was crinkled. It had half a load, but contained everything he felt he needed.

"Follow me," said Amos. "We have two kinds of accommodations here, the bunkroom for the recruits and a few small, private rooms for special guests like you who come here with sterling credentials and a specific purpose. I hear you are from the Point. I'm not giving you any special points for that, but I am impressed with your record of two tours." He didn't have to mention Afghanistan, it was implied. "I also know you got the Silver and they don't give that one for participation."

Adam hadn't thought about that event recently. He had killed four of the enemy to gain access to rescue a wounded soldier when their barracks was overrun by Taliban during his second tour. Seeing four of their own go down was all that was needed to put the enemy on the run. The raid was over quickly and there were no more casualties for Adam's men. The soldier survived his wounds and was returned to the states for treatment and recovery.

For Adam, this episode was ironic. If he had been killed, he would have been nothing more than a statistic. Instead, he succeeded just doing his job and became a hero. What the heck was the difference? There must be thousands of men—yes, some women too—who did the same thing as he, or even more, but weren't lucky enough to live. Besides, in a situation like Adam had faced, you do the right thing because there is no alternative. There was no time to think. He had done what he had to do and it had worked out.

"This is where you will bunk, Adam. Not much but it's private and quiet. There's a sink over here." Amos pointed to a short wall behind the door. "The john and shower facilities are down the hall. I'll let you stow your gear and will come back for you in half an hour. Then, the fun begins."

Adam could see from the look in Amos's eyes that what he was promising was serious, important, and probably not easy. The room was adequate. He had spent a lot of time on the Great Lakes with his family and was accustomed to small, efficient quarters, the kind that could accommodate four comfortably in a 40-foot boat. He hung up the few items that could benefit from being on a hanger, although it didn't look like a few wrinkles mattered much around here. He put his underwear, socks, and a sweater in the drawers, lined up two pair of shoes under the hanging clothes, and stowed his toilet gear on a shelf next to the sink. Just as this task was finished, a knock on the door indicated that Amos was back. It was obvious things ran on time around here. It was now close to 10:00 AM.

"We have a couple of hours before lunch," said Amos. "We'll grab a cup of coffee and head for the ward room and get this started."

Adam followed silently as Amos led him to a small kitchenette with two glass Bunn coffee pots sitting on a warmer next to the small but efficient-looking stove. The coffee smelled a little stale, but slightly stale was better than weak for Adam.

"Black?" Amos looked up at Adam.

"Black."

That settled, Amos filled two cups, handed one to Adam, and led the way out of the room to a bare room across the hall just big enough to accommodate a medium-sized conference table and ten chairs. It had a white board at one end and no windows.

"Have a seat, Adam. Let's get this show on the road."

Adam sat down opposite Amos.

"Adam, I know quite a bit about you—but I suppose you knew that already."

"I do. I guess I am getting used to it," said Adam.

"That's the way it works around here. You don't know a damn thing about me and that is also the way things work around here." Amos sounded like an inquisitor. "All the stuff suitable for your college yearbook and the usual job application is already on the table. Our job here, today and for the rest of the week, is to find out a lot about the other stuff. Don't take offense to anything I ask you or that I say. If you don't want to answer something, that is your prerogative. But, I should warn you, you telling us too little is way worse than telling us too much. The stuff you will not, or cannot say, always comes out, so better to say it now. I am no psychologist …"

That's bull, Adam thought. *What in the hell am I supposed to think he is doing now? And why was Amos the one chosen to talk to me? Okay, everything that will happen this week will be aimed, at least in part, to see if it gets my goat, or if I react like a hot-head. Don't take the bait. Cool it!*

"… just a guy who has been around here for a long time and who has seen a lot of new people. Adam, you are a hell of a well-qualified guy, no question, but if you had to pick out one thing about you that you think is special and that you are proud of, what would it be?"

Adam thought for a moment. No need to hurry, there was plenty of time. He wanted to get it right. "Good, or maybe not so good at times, when I agree to do something, I do it. I try to not bite off more than I can chew, and most of the time I deliver on a promise. You said one, but I would like to add something that I think goes with what I said."

"Let's hear it."

"I respect the people I am asked to lead, and I respect those I follow with essentially no difference in the obligation

I feel toward each. The obligations are different but equal in importance. I have stared down the barrel of a gun and survived. I killed a man because one of us would end up dead and it might as well be him. I know I am going to die some time, not too soon I hope, but *when*, not *if* I do, I want to do it right. I have a pretty good idea about what I can do best and maybe things I can't do at all. I try to use the things I already know about myself to influence what I undertake. If I'm not the smartest guy around, I will be the hardest working."

"Thanks, Adam. What you just told me is what I expected. I appreciate hearing it from you though. This is spy school, and it takes more than being tough and smart to be a good spy. Have you thought about how you fit into that mold?"

Adam almost laughed as he contemplated this question. "Over the years, I have come to realize that I am way too likely to show my emotions on my face. I read about this, and from what I learned it is called the *silent language*. I am afraid I tell people way too much with my body language. People walk up to me unasked and give me directions. The cashier rolls her eyes when she sees me fidgeting while the woman in front of me paws through an overstuffed purse to find a credit card she should have had out before she got in line. Clerks think they need to apologize for keeping me waiting when they really don't need to … and a lot of other things you can guess yourself."

Amos chuckled. "A mark for you when it comes to insight and one against for being transparent. Don't worry, though. The trait you describe is mutable if you know you have it. Anything that really scares you?"

"Lots of things," said Adam. "But for the most part, I think they are things that would scare you or anybody. If it's okay, I will try to answer this in the way you probably meant it."

"Go ahead."

"I have, by way of definition, a classic phobia. I am claustrophobic. For example, when the opportunity arose to go inside a small sightseeing submarine in the Grand Cayman Islands, I simply couldn't do it. My whole family went in a little yellow submarine to look at coral reefs. I would have enjoyed the sights but couldn't deal with the thought of being closed in, so I stayed onshore. Likewise, in the small capsule that is the tourist elevator in the St. Louis Arch, I was bonkers until we reached the open framework of the Arch. Even though I was still in the capsule, I was at ease seeing the open space with supporting girders through the Plexiglas windows. Once on top, I loved it.

"But, on several occasions, I have been able to manage a head MRI. I did this by going in with my eyes closed and keeping them closed for the entire study. I imagined there was lots of space out there and in my mind, there was."

"Sure you're not a shrink yourself, Adam?" chuckled Amos. After another hour of more or less benign back and forth Amos said, "Let's get lunch."

The dining hall was in Building Four, nearest the road and on the other side of the parking lot. It was actually a cafeteria with a well-stocked cold and hot line and a central area with tables each accommodating four or six. Adam had had only juice, a cake donut, and coffee at the complimentary breakfast at the Holiday Inn. He was pretty hungry. The cheeseburger looked good but he opted for stewed tomatoes as a side instead of fries and grabbed a Diet Coke. Amos selected meatloaf, mashed potatoes, and a glass of milk. The room was about half full with twenty-five or so men. Most were Adam's age and younger. A few looked slightly older and definitely tougher. *Instructors?*

As they were eating, Adam pretty much wolfing and Amos chewing at a moderate rate, Amos said, "This afternoon will be easy, at least physically, but it may be the most important thing you learn at this place when it comes to saving your life. And, thanks for being so open this morning. That makes things go a lot better.

"I don't know in detail what you will be up to after you finish here, but that doesn't stop me from speculating. I could be dead wrong, I have been before, but this time I think I've got the situation pegged. From the sketchy briefing I got, I believe you've been tapped for an important job. It has a very short lead time, it will be overseas, you will have at least one partner who will be bona fide CIA, the project will require dealing with assets, and your military background was an important factor in your being selected for the job. That's the long and the short of it."

"You just said a bunch, Amos."

TWENTY-TWO

April 24, Monday

DINNER WAS IN THE SAME CAFETERIA WHERE HE HAD lunch with Amos. The meal was generic: corned beef and cabbage, redskin potatoes, and baby lima beans topped off with cherry pie and coffee. Adam ate early and alone. His first day at The Farm had been interesting and, as Amos had predicted, useful; maybe even essential for survival with what Adam had in store. While Adam ate, he carefully retraced in his mind what happened during the long afternoon session with the polygraph.

Virgil Haines was a technician who specialized in all things pertaining to lie detectors. His shop was in Building One, directly across the parking lot from Building Four. Virgil, as he told Adam to call him, was thin, almost skeletally so, and balding. He wore glasses with perfectly round lenses and heavy, dark, tortoise-shell frames. Glasses like this were both to be looked through and looked at by others. They made a statement.

"For starters," Virgil Haines explained to Adam, "a lie detector measures physiological reactions of the body. When used for the purpose stated by its name, these measurements are recorded while an individual answers questions. It's as simple as that. The instrument is officially called a polygraph. According to official title, I am a forensic psychophysiologist."

Haines stressed that neither the machine nor the tester could determine if the subject was lying; that is, if a specific response was a lie or the truth. The machine merely recorded the body's reactions that were linked to agitation, stimulation, and overall discomfort. The specific physiologic responses recorded are: respiration rate, blood pressure and pulse, and galvanic skin resistance (electro-dermal activity) which is basically sweaty fingertips which are easier to detect and grade but mean the same thing as sweaty palms.

Virgil continued, "The bodily functions we are interested in are sensed using a blood pressure cuff and pulsometer placed on your arm. A slightly inflated soft rubber tube around the chest records respiratory rate. A galvanic skin resistance clip placed on your fingertip records the degree of sweating there. The collected data from these sensors are digitized and compiled on a computer where they are analyzed. This new system is much neater and easier to work with than the old paper rolls and ink stylus."

As he was talking, Virgil Haines, with the skill that came from being an experienced forensic psychophysiologist, placed the paraphernalia he had just finished describing on Adam. No one else was in the room. That was another requirement of this "dance," only the tester and the subject were in the room.

"Just placing this equipment can cause a level of

anxiety," Haines explained, "causing increased response that is essentially extraneous and uninformative. We call it noise. For this test to be accurate, it is necessary to take as much time as needed for these autonomic responses to settle down, normalize, and reach baseline. This can take as long as an hour."

This made Adam realize that the polygraph he was required to take for his job with the General was simply pro forma. He was in and out of the room in forty-five minutes. The tester was polite but looked disinterested and must have been as sure as Adam was when it came to the expected outcome.

Haines continued. "People can beat the polygraph or it can be inconclusive for a variety of reasons, including poor questioning technique. The most likely error on the part of the tester is to ask a question that lacks consequence. Another source of error is a studied non-reaction on the part of the examinee. Some people are born liars and devoid of any semblance of conscience. You can usually tell these people by how they act and what they have done to require having this test. Other techniques for beating the polygraph include sedatives, biting the lip, or even the subject putting nails in his shoes."

Just to make Adam aware that he knew his history, Haines added, "Probably the best polygraph beater our agency has dealt with was Aldrich Ames. He was a pro. He passed three of them while he was pocketing 2.7 million dollars from the Russians for passing secrets. He got caught only because of how he spent his money."

With the tutorial finished, which was probably more to calm than to educate him, Adam spent the next two hours practicing. The goal of the exercise was to have Adam recognize his physiologic responses and strive to feel exactly the same inside when he answered yes to "Is your birthday in December?" when it was in June, as when he said, "Yes, my name is Adam." Those were the simple ones. Many complex and challenging questions followed.

The takeaway from this session was plain and simple: learn to be a better liar!

TWENTY-THREE

April 28, Friday

O N Friday morning, his last day at The Farm, Adam woke at six and saw a note had been slipped under the door. This had been the routine for each of the last three days. These missives told him what the day's activity would be, along with a suggestion on the best thing to wear.

Most of the tests on The Farm had been physical. They included a grueling long-distance run; practice at the shooting range with a familiarization course in handguns, including those he might encounter in a Far East client state of Russia; two sessions on close-order self-defense; and a session in the box.

Each day after breakfast, he was met and taken to the appointed place, or taken from Building Three directly to the day's venue and fed there. The note today told him to report to Building Five at 9:00 AM. Since he would remain in the compound, simply changing buildings, he would not need an escort. He was to wear whatever he thought would be appropriate for classroom work.

It was interesting that the notes never said what he would be doing; only the kind of clothing that would be appropriate. His first session this morning would last until noon. After lunch, Adam would meet with Amos Griggs, who he had not seen since Monday. Adam was very much looking forward to meeting with Amos, the only person he had met at the camp so far who seemed to have a grasp of the bigger picture for Adam.

"Good morning, Major Grant." A man of medium height and probably not much over forty stood alone in a conference room that looked like the twin of where he had met with Amos. Adam guessed the man was Korean.

"My name is Henry Choi," said the man with a disarming half smile. "My expertise, if you can call it that, is having a fair amount of knowledge about the goings on in North Korea."

"Then, you're just the man I should be seeing," said a slightly relieved Adam.

Choi continued. "Before we go any further, I should tell you a bit about myself ..."

Adam chuckled inside and thought, *Mr. Choi, or I bet it will be professor before this is done, I can already tell you something about yourself. You are Korean, smart, and you get right to the point—no nonsense.*

"I was born in Pyongyang in 1977. In 2005, I moved to the South with my parents. I was twenty-eight. We don't call it defection; we were coming home to a Korea where we could live like humans. My father is a professor at the University of Foreign Studies in Seoul. I came to the United States in 2010. For a day job, I am Associate Professor of Far Eastern Studies at American University in D.C. By mutual agreement between the institutions, I am also a CIA recruiter, analyst, and instructor. Have you been to Korea?"

Adam replied, "Before I started at West Point, I took some time off and sort of did a Far East swing, visiting South Korea, Japan, Viet Nam, Thailand, and the Philippines. I was obviously young, and it was quite an adventure for a twenty-year-old traveling mostly alone. That was more than ten years ago, but I don't think things have changed a great deal. I visited China when I was in high school with a student group. That was almost twenty years ago; I know a lot has happened there since my visit."

"That's good, Major."

"Make it Adam."

"Okay. That's a relief. Now you don't have to call me Professor. It's Henry," he said with a chuckle.

After this relaxed introduction, Henry spent the next three hours telling Adam as much as he could absorb, and more, about what he could expect and how he should behave if he were to go to North Korea. The interaction was surreal in that there was never even a hint of the inevitability of Adam's visit. Henry spoke to him as if he were a person who might be going to North Korea on a business trip.

Henry conducted the briefing skillfully; clearly professorial. "I will start telling you some things that you probably already know but, with your permission, I would like to start at the beginning."

"I am all ears. Anything I hear this morning will be useful."

"First, some demographics," began Henry. "The GDP of North Korea is less than twenty billion, an amount that is exceeded by even the smallest state in the U.S., and is less than two percent of the GDP of the State of New York. The North Koreans spend nearly a quarter of their GDP on the military, which numbers about four million including active military and reserve units out of a population of just under twenty-six million. The numbers go on in the same dismal way; so you get the idea North Korea is a poor country that spends a hell of a lot on the military."

Adam asked, "Are there strengths and weaknesses in the North Korean military?"

Henry replied, "Good question. North Korea's military is almost totally offensive. They have up to sixteen nuclear warheads, something that has received a lot of publicity recently. More important, they are developing long-range-missile launch capability with help from Iran and possibly China. They are said to have more than 10,000 tube artillery units and more than 2,000 rocket-launching devices, all aimed at the South. The country could be overrun and conquered by a conventional force in days, but not before it launched one or possibly more nuclear warheads and bombarded Seoul with an artillery force that could kill half a million people. Attacking North Korea with conventional forces would be like taking down a hornet's nest with a baseball bat. You will win but you will get stung and stung badly. And, most believe a preemptive nuclear attack carried out against North Korea is unthinkable because of the effect it would have on the rest of the world."

"I appreciate getting your insight, Henry. I must say that this confirms what I believe about the situation in North Korea and what the people in D.C. think too. I am told that malnutrition is widespread."

Henry's face clouded. "Reliable sources say that fully one third of children are undernourished and suffer from rash and diarrhea. Adam, all of us on the peninsula started with the same DNA, but we are no longer the same people. The population in the North is significantly smaller than those in the South, but that is only the physical difference. The sense of decency, responsibility, and honor has been purged from much of the population in the North by a cruel and despotic regime that has assumed full power and, in their own minds, invincibility. Whoa I'd better get off the soapbox."

"I understand, but how are relationships on a one-to-one, personal level?"

"Another good question. My mom and dad kept their sanity and values intact and left the North twelve years ago; emotionally intact but not by much. North Korea dictates hairstyle, has a farcical election every five years, and has its own calendar that says the year is 105, coinciding with the birth year of Leader Kim-Il-sung. Criminals are dealt with by going back three generations or more when meting out punishment. The tallest building in the city of Pyongyang is a hotel at one thousand feet. It was begun in 1987 and remains unfinished and unoccupied today.

"Much of the country is without electricity. There is no available Internet for the population, only intranet. Bookstores and libraries have few books and those they have are mainly for the purpose of propaganda. I'll stop here. You can imagine the rest—it is all bad."

"What about the labor camps?

"There are probably six of them, with as many as 20,000 people interred. Simply displeasing the Leader is sufficient to be sent to a camp, and many high-ranking officials have ended up in one. The brutal treatment in these hell holes has been well documented and has been censured by the UN in a three-hundred-page report that, as you might expect, had absolutely no impact."

"I get the picture, Henry. What's the bottom line?"

"Right," said the professor resignedly. "It is this, Adam. There are still a few good folks left. My parents couldn't have been the only ones. It is my understanding, unofficially; there are CIA assets in the country, not many but a few. North Korea has a small export industry, including clothing and apparel manufacture. To be successful, these operations must be run by people with sense—and anyone with sense has to recognize that the country is a mess. The North also has a special durable cloth called vinylon. It is the national fiber. It was invented by a Korean in 1939 and, after World War II, he defected to the North. The idiot!"

This last information was very specific. Is it significant? Adam thought so.

Adam could see a large, round clock behind Henry. It was almost noon. "How should we end this, Henry?"

"How about this? I expect you are doing this in preparation for a visit that I don't know about and don't want to know about. You are a smart guy and have been around. You will meet several people in North Korea; some might be snakes who will do you in. Be careful. Listen to the assets on the ground. They are acting not simply as mercenaries, as is so often the case. There are actually some patriots. Be careful and be well." With that Henry stood and said, "Now, I take off my Superman cape and drive back to D.C. where I teach a night class. Nice meeting you, Adam."

"Likewise," Adam said.

Adam entered the conference room in Building Three. It was precisely 1:00 PM. Amos was in the same chair he had occupied for their first meeting; Adam took his same seat opposite. Amos did not get up. *I'll be damned if I speak first,* thought Adam. *This is his party.* He silently looked at Amos; it almost felt adversarial.

The old man broke the silence. "How did you like the week, Major?"

"Compared to what?"

"Oh. It was that much fun, was it?"

"Yeah, except for that box they put me in to see if I had

enough balls to deal with my claustrophobia. And don't tell me that is part of the routine."

"I am sorry, Adam. You are right. It is not part of the routine and you would not have been disqualified whatever the outcome. You see, I am a sadistic old bastard and I have found the best way to find out about a man is to attack him in his most vulnerable place. If he fails, he can still get a B or even a B+, depending on the other stuff. If he passes that test, he gets an A or an A+ on the same grounds. We don't tell people their grades, and that's good because who in the hell are we to judge? But, I'll tell you this, you passed—and not with a B+."

They talked for about an hour, but there really wasn't much more to say. Amos finally said, "This about wraps things up for us here, Adam. You are welcome to stay the night, or if you want, you can head back home. You could be back in D.C. by dinnertime."

"I think I'll do that. Amos, thanks for almost everything."

Amos Griggs knew what was being omitted in the thanks, but he was glad he had put Adam in the box. This guy was just too good not to be tested to the limits.

On the drive home, Adam decided to call Brenda. He would set up a date night for the following evening. Poor girl, he knew she wouldn't be busy and Adam was feeling guilty that he would probably be absent for the rest of her pregnancy. He wondered what he could do to make sure Chad got home in time.

TWENTY-FOUR

April 29, Saturday

ADAM HOPPED OUT OF THE BLACK CHEVY UBER IN front of Brenda's apartment. He told the driver to wait, and bounded up the steps and into the foyer where he rang Brenda's apartment. She buzzed back. He knew she would be down in a minute so he waited.

Brenda came at him with a scowl. Not a real one but the kind a girl puts on her face when she catches a boy being too much of a boy, showing off. "Adam, you rascal. You know our agreement. We meet at the restaurant and we go Dutch."

"Hush, Brenda. In your delicate condition, you deserve all of the solicitude you can get and, my dear, that's *my* prerogative."

"Well, Major Grant, I'll excuse you this time, but please don't make a habit of it."

"As you were, Mrs. Gale."

The car took them to their favorite spot. After they ordered Adam started. "Brenda, I am going on assignment and this will be our last dinner for a while."

Brenda looked squarely at Adam, showing the colors of a military wife. "Not back to …"

"No, Brenda. Not that." She was obviously referring to Afghanistan, where Chad was. "Just some administrative stuff. Think of me as shouldering a task rather than using that other part of my anatomy while I sit at a desk. I'll tell you about it when I get back—it's no big deal."

The rest of the evening was pleasant and customary, although Adam could sense the disappointment that Brenda felt in losing her "second soldier." She assured Adam that she would have plenty of support. Her mother and sister were coming for separate visits, and she had become friendly with two military wives in her building, both of whom had young children. She told Adam her due date was four months off, in early September, and he had better be back for the christening because she and Chad were counting on Adam being the child's godfather.

Continuing the chivalrous role, Adam paid for dinner and they Ubered back to Brenda's apartment, where he escorted her to the foyer. After a brotherly hug, Adam put Brenda on the elevator, and left the building. This was just the first thing he owed Brenda and Chad; there was more and he would manage it somehow.

As soon as the elevator doors closed, a new existence began for Adam; He was now fully engaged in his assignment, and deadly serious.

TWENTY-FIVE

May 1, Monday

ON SATURDAY EVENING, ADAM HAD RECEIVED A
cryptic message telling him, not asking, to report
to Room 306, new building at Langley, at 9:00 AM
Monday. There was no signature, only a vague indication
that the message was sent by the Personnel Office. He
would be starting the week at Langley. Adam was ready,
but for what?

After the usual showing of ID, Adam was told to take the
elevator on the right to the third floor. Leaving the elevator
and turning right Adam could see from the progression of
room numbers he was going the right way.

The door to Room 306 was open. The only person he recognized at the table was Erin O'Leary. Adam had wondered

if this woman would be a one-off, a screener who had done her job and would move on. He was happy to see a familiar face, especially one that belonged to someone Adam had decided was a classy and capable individual. There were four other people in the room.

"Welcome, Major Grant," said Erin. Then, with the formal title acknowledged and getting down to business, Erin O'Leary continued. "Adam, I would like you to meet the core support team for a project that you are familiar with and, more than that, you are effectively responsible for: the effort to accomplish a regime change in North Korea to forestall what is being considered an imminent nuclear threat to the United States."

Adam was pleased that the necessary hush-hush seemed to have been done away with, at least in this room. He was relieved and felt exhilarated, but he retained an impassive look. *Let's see what they have before committing. It looks like I will have some say, or maybe even a lot of responsibility, when it comes to how this moves forward.*

"At the start, I would like to re-state that the mission we are embarking on is to do all in our power to keep the North Korean regime from launching a nuclear attack on the United States. Both conventional arms and a preemptive nuclear strike have been ruled out. We will assume the responsibility for averting this threat, which is actually Kim Il-un himself. Our goal is to end the reign of Kim Il-un while leaving North Korea and the rest of the world intact. In other words: we are responsible for making an omelet without breaking the egg. This will be accomplished by using whatever means necessary. Is this your understanding?" Erin scanned the room and saw assent on everyone's face. She continued. "Let's start with introductions. First, I would like all of you to welcome Major Adam Grant— West Point grad, two tours in Afghanistan, Silver Star, and currently working in D.C., but now on loan to us. The rest of you know each other, but for Adam's benefit, introduce yourselves and describe your role." Turning to her right, Erin indicated who should start.

"My name is Sam Bradford. I've been here for twelve years. My job is logistics and, as you all know, that covers a lot of sins, so I will need lots of guidance and cooperation."

"I'm Phil Park, Operations. I have knowledge of the assets in the North." Adam knew those few words said a lot.

"My name is Ellen Hirschman. I have twenty years' experience at the United Nations and am familiar with North Korea's UN observer representatives. I remain in contact with several who hold important positions in the People's Republic."

Finally, the youngest of the group said, "I'm Eddie Freeman. My gig is everything electronic, especially communications and location."

Erin explained her role. "I am here representing Operations and have been designated leader of the group. I will be working closely with Major Grant ..."

That's good news, thought Adam.

"... who will be the point man cooperating with all of us; including helping each of us as we continue to work with our own support teams if necessary. We will remain a functioning team until the project reaches a successful conclusion. But, before I answer any questions, I would like you to hear from Major Grant." Erin O'Leary turned to Adam. "Major Grant, will you provide us an outline of your plan?" Before he could start, she added, "Before you hear the details of this plan, I can assure all of you that the concept has been approved at the highest, but unspecified, levels. The execution, and I don't necessarily expect this to be meant literally, has been put in our hands, subject to final approval from appropriate levels in our own organization. It goes without saying that everything we say and do in this regard is to be treated as Classified at the highest level and all of our communications are to be treated as confidential. Adam …"

They were officially using first names now. "Thank you, Erin. I will be brief. Erin has already told you why we are embarking on this project and its desired outcome. I will do my best to provide an outline of how we propose to accomplish this. We will install a high-level American defector, an imposter, into North Korea. This person will have instantly recognized credibility in that he will be an officer in the U.S. military, a West Point graduate, and an ethnic Korean. This 'defector' will renounce his U.S. citizenship and denounce our country as racist; belligerent; dominating; and falsely projecting democracy and equality while creating a self-ish, capitalistic society that aims at world domination and enslavement of anyone it can control. Have I said enough about how much this guy will say he hates America? No offense to the women here, but I do think this fake defector needs to be a man."

Assessing the small audience, Adam saw no surprise, only moderate interest. He continued. "The defector will manage to get close to Kim, who we know has an affin-ity for celebrity and loves to show off. You may recall his meetings with Dennis Rodman that the media ate up. The proximity that we believe the defector can attain will make it possible for him, with help from locals, to deal with Kim at the appropriate time. Disabling the Leader and confining him under the control of new leadership would be ideal but not a requisite. This pudgy, little fellow murders relatives with impunity and subjects tens of thousands of his people to slave labor, starvation, and torture. If he 'checked out,' whose conscience will it be on?" This was a 007 moment that Adam thought needed no further explanation.

Adam continued. "There is a significant back-story to this project and it starts with the need to recruit a defector.

We already have a candidate. I say 'we' literally because he doesn't know it yet. He will be contacted when this group finishes its preliminary business. The project will begin with assets on the ground that must be mobilized to identify and contact sympathetic people in leadership positions within the North Korean government and military. This includes the need to enlist at least one high-ranking official with the prestige and influence to move forward with a post-Kim leadership at least on a temporary basis until there are elections. The new government would aim at pacifying the country, freeing political prisoners, feeding the starving children, and returning the country to the family of nations. As this newly constituted country is being created, the U.S. will provide a large amount of food and other humanitarian aid and we expect there will be an outpouring from other countries as well. Whatever we spend will be a pittance compared with trying to heal the aftermath of a nuclear assault."

The silence was broken by Sam Bradford. "When do we get started?"

TWENTY-SIX

May 1, Monday

T HE INITIAL MEETING OF WHAT THEY NOW CALLED THE Trojan Horse Project continued for almost an hour. It was mostly everybody getting comfortable with the people they would be working with closely for the duration of the mission. Erin let the meeting wind down at its own pace. Before she released the group, Erin promised they would reconvene soon, probably sometime later that week. She asked them to let her know if they would be leaving town and to give thought to the role they might be expected to play. This was a good group, all pros. They had heard just enough of the plan to come up with some ideas about how they could accomplish their part of the project.

As the room emptied, Adam looked at Erin. The look on his face was complex and purposefully unreadable, something new for him. He was searching for something to say.

"We've got a tiger by the tail." He was immediately sorry for mouthing this trite remark. Acknowledging this he said, "Sorry, Erin, that doesn't even approach the situation."

"Don't apologize, Adam. I may look like I have it all together, but I feel the same way; only I might say, and only to you, I feel like I've got my guts on the table."

This broke the ice. "That's enough of the graphic sharing, young lady. Let's get down to business."

The down-to-business part, at least at the start, was solely on Adam's plate, but he wanted Erin's input. The only chance for a plan like this to get legs was to have the team solidly onboard. "Erin," he began, "none of this is going to work until we have our defector. I have someone in mind but convincing him may be something I can't do alone. Let me tell you what I have in mind and give me your input."

"Fine," Erin said. "But I don't work well on an empty stomach. Let's get some lunch and in the process, let's find something better than Starbucks."

"Your call," said Adam.

"We can go to a place I know on old Dominion, about ten minutes from here. I'll drive and drop you off back here to pick up your car. For the record, this is a working lunch and we will be on the clock." Then, as an afterthought, Erin said, "But if it's alright with you, I may enjoy it. Okay?"

Could she be flirting? Nah, no way, Adam concluded. Then, contradicting himself, he continued the repartee. "As my mother would have said, especially if she had met you, don't turn down lunch with a good-looking spy." *Don't get giddy*, Adam thought. Then he recognized it was just an automatic reaction, a letting down of his guard after a tense encounter; like the reflexive gallows humor that happened with his men after almost getting their heads blown off in Afghanistan.

J. Gilbert's Wood-Fired Steak Restaurant looked good; it wasn't a chain. It had the pseudo sophistication that would attract a boy taking a girl to dinner before the prom. The atmosphere was dark, especially for the middle of the day, and the booths were private. Perfect. Adam wanted to go into more detail about the recruiting process and he suspected Erin could come up with something useful. This lunch could be the first concrete step in moving the plan forward. Adam had thought about this so much in the last three weeks that he had a hard time realizing he had never told anybody how he had planned for the events to unfold. Erin must have sensed this.

"Adam, you look like you are about to burst. Out with it. We need to get the show on the road."

"You're right!" Adam suspected this smart lady was right most of the time. "Let's order first. Since this is a steak house, I am going to have …" He glanced at the menu. "… the flat-iron steak with wine sauce, mashed potatoes, and roasted asparagus; and a Diet Coke."

When the server came, Adam ordered first because he, indeed, was bursting and wanted to start as soon as possible.

"Just so you don't think I am only a salad girl, I am going to have the same except with iced tea." The server jotted down their order and started to head off.

"Oh, miss," Adam caught the server's attention while she was still within earshot and said, "Is the lump crab, roasted shrimp, and mushroom appetizer as good as it sounds?"

"Absolutely, even better!" the pleasant young woman replied.

"We'll have that appetizer—and put it on my bill." They had already decided to go Dutch on the ride over.

With this taken care of, Erin said, "Let's hear it."

"Here is what I am proposing. We dangle this super-credible defector in front of Kim Il-un. Kim will adopt him like he did Dennis Rodman, and will use our guy as a propaganda tool, rubbing our nose in his defection. The defector will then act as a lightning rod for the already disaffected members of the inner circle, both military and political, who we know exist, and possibly in pretty big numbers. For our plan to work, it will be good, or more likely necessary, to have these people identified ahead of time and onboard as soon as possible. This will mean pulling out all the stops to get this group identified, confirmed as willing, and informed of the role they will play."

Erin broke in. "I get it for the phony defector. It won't be easy, but we can do it. How do we mobilize the North Koreans to help?"

"That is where your operations team comes in," explained Adam. "We send a small team, maybe only two people, to North Korea to make contact with assets there. They will have already been briefed by their handlers, that will be Phil, who will urge them to make a list of potential partners in this enterprise. Our small team will consolidate these efforts, which will take about a week, in Pyongyang. With this team mobilized, on our signal, the defector will arrive on the scene and events will start to roll."

Erin asked, "What does the front team do when the defector arrives?"

"The front team leaves for home—but doesn't come here. Instead they will stay in the South to remain close and to provide support for the defector. And this is where your shop comes in. We will need *Star Wars* caliber communication and we will need an exit strategy for our defector, at the conclusion or earlier in case of an emergency."

"How does all of this come down?" was Erin's logical next question.

"Kim will be disabled when the time is right. It could happen at a big event, such as a missile launch; or possibly a public event, where Kim will want to show off the defector from the U.S. *Disabled* is used here a euphemism. The plan calls for Kim to be either killed or impounded. This will be messy, chaotic, and quick. Success will depend on having a cadre of dependable locals, perfect timing, and luck. We are offering Kim a Trojan horse and we plan for it to bite him."

Erin added, "Those Greeks who went into the enemy camp in the belly of the horse were pretty gutsy. Do we have someone like that?"

"Yes and no. We have identified the prototype and have picked out a candidate who fits the profile. Our job now is to approach him and convince him to do the job. That is step number one, and it is definitely our biggest hurdle."

"Who is it?"

"His name is John Yuen. He is a West Point graduate, and he is Korean. He comes from a military family. His father is a Bird colonel, and his grandfather served in the South Korean Army during the war. He was at West Point a year behind me. He is a good student, excelled at intramural athletics, and has a softer side. He was in the Glee Club for three years."

"Any idea about whether he will do it?"

"Nothing specific, only circumstantial. West Pointers, by and large, are gung-ho—and both his father and grandfather served in the military."

"What would be the most likely reason for him to say no?" Erin had hit the weakest point. Adam had wrestled with this.

"The reason he, or anyone for that matter, would say no is that the truth behind his defection would be a secret; which means his parents will be devastated and his friends will likely desert him. Some might say to the press that they had expected something like this from him all along— nonsense, most will be shocked and even disbelieving, but people are people. His parents will probably, in their hearts, know that something is not as it seems, but we will not be able to ally their concerns. Even after it is done, it is likely the truth will remain buried. If the project succeeds, he may be able to tell his family, but they will have to remain silent. It is essential that our government is not blamed. A tough sell!"

Erin now popped the next logical question. "How widely known is this scheme?"

"It's hard to say. I shared a what-if with General Wieland, but we were both careful to talk around things. He shared with me his concerns, and told me what went down at the National Security Council meeting with the President. They are all worried; maybe scared as hell."

"And the President?"

"He is officially out of the loop. Anything beyond that is above my pay grade."

"Anybody else know?"

"Orville McPherson, the head of DNI, knows something is up. He has been in contact with your boss, Bob Zinsky, which is why you are here."

"Do I detect a heavy dose of plausible deniability?" Erin posed the question but she already knew the answer.

"Definitely."

Erin looked down at the empty plate that had held the strawberry cheesecake she had for dessert. It was about the best she had ever eaten. She nodded yes to the server who was offering her a third cup of coffee. "What is the very next thing we should do?"

The ball was back in his court, but Adam was ready. "First, we should get back with the team and get them working."

"How?"

"Okay. You asked for it. I would like the Agency to fly us down to Fort Sam Houston where Captain Yuen is teaching at the Medical Field Service School. By 'us' I mean I want you to go along. You pack a lot of cred. Before that, we should meet with the team. I have some ideas about what I want them to do, but it is up to them on how it will be accomplished. The first overseas venture will be the advance team to mobilize assets and the local support. I would like to take the lead, but I will need a partner."

"I would like to apply," said Erin.

Ignoring that for now, Adam continued. "There will be a lot of details to be managed. This will be a complex operation, not like D-Day, just the opposite. Not many people involved and done in the dark, but dependent on total precision for the few delicate working parts."

The lunch crowd had long since cleared. The two had been oblivious of anything but their conversation.

"You really want to go?" Adam finally responded to Erin's offer.

"Yes."

"Then, I guess the answer is yes." Adam was beginning to get the idea that Erin had a great deal of authority when it came to this project.

"Can you meet with the team soon?" asked Erin.

"Yes."

"When?"

"Let's meet at 9:00 AM on Wednesday." After a pause, he added, "We'd better get out of here before they start charging rent—or hand us a dinner menu!"

TWENTY-SEVEN

May 3, Wednesday

WEDNESDAY MORNING IT WAS MUCH COOLER AND raining hard. The temperature was in the fifties, well below normal. Every time he woke up to rain, Adam remembered what his grandmother had said, "Starts before seven; quits before eleven." As a child, he thought that was some kind of magical formula. Then he learned that weather systems usually move from the west to the east, unless it was a hurricane ripping northward up the East Coast.

When he arrived at Room 306, it was five minutes before nine. The group was already assembled. Adam was only okay at remembering names, but faces were etched in his brain, which was good for dealing with people but not when it came to greeting them. Because of the special nature of this group and the importance of this project, Adam had both the faces, names, and responsibilities fully memorized.

Erin started the meeting. "The first order of business today is to develop a plan for getting two of the team to Pyongyang. By that, I mean beginning preparation for departure and for maintaining support while they are there. This needs to be completed soon. Adam and I will be going." She looked at Adam as if for concurrence and reinforcement. "We plan to leave for Pyongyang in two weeks, on or about May 18th. Once there, we plan to have our work finished within seven to ten days. For this to happen, it will take contributions from all of you."

The group was focused; even excited to hear what would come next. This project had more far-reaching consequence than they were used to dealing with. People think the CIA is a thrill a minute, but that simply is not so. This would be a big deal—a welcomed high-level effort for everyone in the room.

"Here are some parameters," Erin continued. "Our cover will be that we are in Pyongyang to do business. Neither of us will be U.S. citizens; we will be traveling with assumed names, country of origin to be determined. Our real purpose while there is to meet with local assets who have been recruited to cooperate with the CIA and who will be informed of our visit in advance. This asset group will tell us about government and military officials who are intent on bringing down the regime before Kim commits whatever horrendous act of nuclear destruction he has in mind. Let's consider that the essence of our effort is to mobilize an effective home front and spur them to action. We will meet these assets when it is possible for them to do so.

"This is only the first part of an intricate puzzle, where all of the parts must function properly, fit perfectly, and be in place at the precise time for us to be successful at inserting the 'defector,' who will, with the help of locals, disable Kim. If any part of the plan fails, it all fails. Let's get started."

Erin scanned the table, looking for the first to respond.

As she expected, it was Sam Bradford. "Erin, why don't I kick this off? I had a hunch things would be going down like this, and I have some ideas. Actually, I put an insertion plan together a couple of years ago. It never happened, but I kept the dope on it and it looks like a lot of what I have already done will work here."

"Tell us."

"It goes something like this: two people are visiting North Korea to negotiate a clothing manufacturing deal. I chose this line of business because textile is one of the country's few successful export items. The two people in this scenario are a man and a woman. The man represents a manufacturer in the Netherlands, who will be introducing a line of health and action wear. The woman represents a large retail operation in Germany that also exports to North America."

"And?" Erin took advantage of a slight pause to emphasize to Sam that she was hanging on his words.

"They have selected North Korea because labor costs are about one tenth of those in Europe; and more importantly, the clothing will be made out of vinylon. Vinylon, as you probably already know, is a fabric developed in North Korea and is something the country is proud of. It essentially replaced cotton, which is scarce there. The fabric is tough and long-wearing. It can be more difficult to work with than cotton, and it doesn't hold dye well, but it is particularly resistant to heat, which is important for the product we will be pitching."

"Why is this important?" Erin asked.

"There is a damn good reason. Foreigners don't just drop into 'Kim country' to have the pleasure of working with people beholden to a ruthless regime. There must be a purpose and our opportunistic couple is there is to take advantage of a unique fabric. They will be ordering several million units of manufactured garments and other cloth components that will be used to make clothing and other items that will allow for the application of focal 'therapeutic' heat. This treatment will be used for everything from psoriasis to deep vein thrombosis. North Korean Vinylon is the name of the manufacturer we will approach to supply the vinylon products. They will not be in on the gig, so our duo has to know their onions."

"If the manufacturer is not in on this, will he be likely to check up on these folks by going online?" asked Adam.

"Absolutely. We already have a complete online cover for the Dutch company Wearable Therapeutics. This website will feature our dynamic duo and some other people from the company, a picture of the plant, the story of the concept etc., etc. There will be contact information and our team will be ready to respond appropriately. But, since North Korea is essentially off the grid and relies on its own propaganda intranet, this may be overkill."

"Do we have a sales pitch for the product?" asked Erin.

"We already have a start, including brochures, but Adam and Erin will need patterns, sales projections, business cards ... the whole nine yards. We will take care of all that."

"Who will we be?" Erin wondered aloud.

"You will be Lisa Park, and you live in Germany. Adam, you will be Jan deFever; you live in Amsterdam, where the factory is located.

"What if they call Amsterdam directly, to check?" Erin was being the thorough school teacher again.

"Any phone calls to Wearable Therapeutics will be routed to a special operator at the U.S. Embassy in The Hague. They will be transferred to our team at Langley, who will be your factory back home. This team will be able to produce any company representative they ask for up, including the president, who will vouch for Lisa Park and Jan deFever. He will be very enthusiastic about the venture, which he hopes will be just the start of bigger things. The Koreans will not be able to track these garments because they have yet to reach the retail market. The products they will be working on will be a first.

"To complete the logistics, we will provide the appropriate passports, other identification, and travel arrangements. You will fly from here to Amsterdam with your own identities. Once in Amsterdam, you will assume your new identities. This will be the origination of your trip in so far as it is trackable. With your new identities, you will first fly to Beijing on KLM; and from there you will take Koryo Airline to Pyongyang—we can't guarantee it won't be a thirty-year-old Tupolev."

"Sounds good, Sam," said Erin. "Do any of you have any questions or comments?"

"I do," said Adam. "What about clothes?"

"Any specific question on that?" replied Sam.

"I bought some LB Tech Chinos at Costco yesterday, along with a few other things."

"Bring everything you intend to pack here—actually, bring the suitcase already packed exactly as you will be taking it—and we will replace the labels. No quicker way to blow your cover as a Dutchman than to have all of your labels be something you can get at Costco or Wal-Mart; that is, if your clothing tastes are like Jack Reacher. Adam, you are starting to ask questions like a spy, and in these walls, I say that as a compliment. I should also tell you both that not more than five minutes after you leave your hotel rooms, agents will go through every inch of the room, including all of your luggage."

"Bang up job, Sam," complimented Erin. "There may be a few last-minute details but this sounds like it's most of it. Who's next?"

Phil Park was ready. "I'm good to go to Pyongyang any day. I will meet with four principal assets and brief them on the intent of our plan but not the details. No point in having the details out too soon and take the chance of being compromised. Of course, I will make sure they are onboard before giving you two the go ahead." He nodded to the head of the table where Erin and Adam sat.

Beyond that, there was not much more for Phil to say. The assets were not identified by name or position, as was the custom. The anonymity of these people was for their personal safety and the longer they stayed that way, the more useful they were. The responsibility for their being reliable was entirely on the shoulders of the handler, Phil Park in this case. He took this responsibility seriously.

"One more thing," said Phil. "You should know that the agents will find you. Don't in any way try to contact them. They will do everything they can to help, but remember, they can only do so much."

"Go it," Adam answered for both of them.

"I will give you the go ahead as soon as we clear this upstairs, but it will be sooner rather than later. Thanks, Phil," said Erin. "Ellen, what do you have for us?"

"From this end, it is a damn sight more complicated than changing some labels. No offense, Sam."

"None taken. I like to change labels."

Ellen Hirschman continued. "My best connection is Lee Wu-jin the North Korean Foreign Minister, who I have dealt with at the UN for nearly ten years. He is smart, effective, and pretty much Westernized as far as his tastes go. We have had some fairly intense conversations about how things are at home. He keeps hoping that the leadership will come to its senses, but realizes with Kim Il-un the country is 'on a downward spiral.' Those were his words the last time we spoke. He is definitely ripe. I would love to get him over here, but on such short notice that just isn't in the cards. I can alert him with our own communication methods but that is all; no details. Erin and Adam, it will be up to you to meet with him when you are in Pyongyang. Can your guys help, Phil?"

Phil nodded. "Yes, there is a line of communication. I will make sure it will be tapped before I sign off on this."

Ellen Hirschman completed her report. "That's about all I have. I sure wish there was a way to get Wu over, but that isn't going to happen. If I tried, it would raise enough of a stink that the whole operation could be lost."

All eyes turned to Eddie. "Hey, it's finally my turn! You all know electronics sucks in that godforsaken country, but we have a work around. We will place—actually, there are already several of them there—two additional drones flying at 30,000 feet over Pyongyang. They are programmed to transmit signals at a frequency and with a channel that is uniquely matched with communication devices that will be on all of our personnel starting with the advance team and then the Trojan horse when he is inserted. These signals can be used for communication and for location by GPS. We can get them small enough to fit in the ear canal, the heel of a shoe, in a belt buckle, and even a class ring, from the University of the Netherlands, of course." This led to a glance in Sam's direction.

"Can these be detected with a metal detector or by causing frequency jamming?" asked Adam.

"No. These are made with a 3D printer out of new material now being used for dental implants that are replacing gold crowns. The material is strong, does not show up on metal testing, and does not affect transmission. As for jamming, we are working so far outside the usual frequencies there will be no problem with this."

"Sounds good, Eddie," said Erin. "How long will this take?"

"Not exactly off the shelf, but we have all of the parts, and 3D printing is a bloody miracle. We'll need the people to get casts for their ear molds, and Sam, if you can share the suitcase with us, we can put devices in the shoes and belt buckles. Adam, we need your ring size."

As the group filed out, Erin said to Adam, "When do you want to meet tomorrow?"

"How about 10:00 AM in your office?"

"Why so late?"

Here it comes, Adam thought. *The secrets that get shared out of necessity change the way we treat even those people who we trust most and who we most want to trust us. How much should I tell her? What do I have to tell her? The General and I are on a strictly PD basis.* "I have to stop by the office to see General Wieland about a godfather thing."

"Not the Mafia, I hope!" joked Erin.

"No, the real thing, the family thing. I am standing in for a buddy in Afghanistan. His wife is due with their first child in four months. She just asked me to be godfather and I agreed, but what I really want to do for her, and the dad, is get him home before for the big event. He has been there for almost six months. I am going to ask a favor of the General." Adam didn't want to answer any questions about what the General knew or didn't know about Project Trojan Horse.

He didn't have to. Erin didn't ask. "See you tomorrow, Adam."

TWENTY-EIGHT

May 4, Thursday

A DAM WALKED INTO HIS OFFICE AT THE PENTAGON AT eight thirty. If a replacement had been assigned, he wasn't there. Adam's office looked the same as he had left it. Maybe the new guy wasn't onboard yet. It had only been three weeks, although to Adam it felt more like a year. He thought about what it would be like when he returned, if he returned. Looking around, he wondered if it could ever be the same. This CIA stuff was something else. You work in a civilized setting with people who, at least on the surface, seemed normal. In other ways, the job seemed to have seriousness similar to Afghanistan but without the daily worry of staying alive.

Adam went directly into his office. Cissy was not at her desk in the reception area between the General's large office and Adam's small one. He had been waiting almost a half hour. Now that he knew the way, he knew he could get to

Langley in thirty minutes, but that would cut it pretty close for his meeting with Erin. Getting anxious, he walked to the door of his office and looked out. Cissy was now at her desk.

"I wasn't sure you still worked here!" Adam kidded.

"I was at the copy machine with this big load." The person they all thought of as Miss Efficiency pointed to what looked like a ream of paper next to her computer.

"Just kidding, Cissy."

"Hey, thanks for the candy, Major. But, it caused me to do two things."

"What?"

"Buy more and not share!" Cissy smiled as she said this. "It's about the best chocolate I ever tasted."

"Glad you liked it. Where's the General?"

"Not sure. He didn't say anything about being late and he even said he was looking forward to meeting with you this morning."

"The new guy here yet?"

"Yes, but his office is down the hall. You should feel honored that the General didn't want to put someone in your office and have it look like they were replacing you. He wants you back. The new guy is okay—but just a useful placeholder."

That made Adam feel good. It also made him feel a bit guilty for thinking that his new assignment was more fulfilling than working for the General. He both liked and respected General Wieland; the older man had become many things to Adam, including friend, boss, and mentor. In this relationship of mutual respect, Adam believed that both mentor and mentee benefited.

He checked his watch and realized he would not be seeing the General today. It was nine thirty and he had to be on his way to Langley. "Tell the General I was here, Cissy, and ask him when he has time to meet with me; then let me know. I prefer to talk with him personally, but that's his option. See ya, Cissy."

Cissy nodded. "See ya, Major." After a pause, she added, "We miss ya. Hurry back."

———

The small office that Adam entered for today's meeting was neat, orderly, and looked efficient. It was about what Adam expected to see when he entered Erin's lair. It projected the personality of its well-organized tenant. Except for its comely occupant, the best thing about this office was an almost ceiling-to-floor undraped window that looked out to a wide lawn and garden that was framed with an urban forest. *She wasn't the director, but she has the same view,* thought Adam. Considering all that went on in this building, the architects and builders had added every touch possible to soften the image of a place whose mission definitely had a hard edge.

"Welcome to the 150 square feet of my home away from home."

I wonder where she actually does live. "Ready to get down to business?" he said, more to himself than to Erin.

"Absolutely, let's do it," said Erin. "I expect you have a plan to get started with John Yuen." When Adam didn't respond immediately she said, "We're not exactly *The Publishers Weekly Sweepstakes* giving away five thousand dollars a week for life. How do we break the ice and then take the leap to get him onboard?"

Adam had thought about how to approach a fellow officer with this proposition for so long and so intensely, he should have been nothing short of eloquent. But after this specific request from Erin, he was almost at a loss for words. He had to start somewhere. "We are tasked with asking a man to forsake just about everything he believes in and loves; and, in the process, he could also die. I can't think of anything that could be worse. On the other hand, he will be committing what could go down as one of the greatest acts of heroism ever performed by a U.S. citizen. Not much could be better."

"This will still be a hard sell, Adam. If I were in his shoes, I would say, 'Why me?' You have described the very worst and the very best ends of the scenario. What's in between?"

"The mitigating circumstances are mainly that the event is time limited. I grant you, it is not much different than having a root canal without anesthesia, but it does have an end. John McCain must have felt this way when he endured thumb screws at the Hanoi Hilton. It also occurred to me that no matter how much pain his family will endure, they will probably suspect that there is more to the picture than what they are seeing or being told. In their own hearts and minds, they would know that their son is not what he is being portrayed to be. This isn't a lot of solace, but it is some."

"Anything else?"

"Our defector could die, or worse, be captured. The problem is that we are operating in the twilight zone of plausible deniability. The U.S. is planning a regime change, even if it means assassinating a foreign leader. People know it but don't want to know it and it looks like they don't ever intend to admit anything. That's dicey stuff. Funny, if Reagan had killed Muammar Gaddafi when we dropped bombs on his compound, it would be called retaliation for an act of war—sort of. It would be impersonal and considered a good thing, kind of like shooting Osama. If our defector sticks a knife in Kim's ribs, that's assassination—murder—not what we do. If a North Korean patriot takes out the leader, it is patriotism. If we do it, it is an act of war against all convention. In any case, the result is the same but the implications are totally different. We are a funny people. Erin, we have to admit that we are dealing in a grey zone and we must simply do the best we can."

The looked at each other in silence. Erin said, "Adam, are we starting to say the same things over and over again, trying to turn something bad into something good on its own?"

"You're right," Adam replied. "How soon can we see John Yuen, and how is he going to be prepared?"

"I'll get that done from here," Erin said.

"My dance card's empty, so just let me know," Adam replied.

TWENTY-NINE

May 4, Thursday

THE CALL FROM CISSY FRIEND WAS GUT-WRENCHING.
It came as he was heading for his car after meeting
with Erin. "Adam, General Wieland is dead." Cissy's
voice was barely in control. Adam knew Cissy was at the
end of her rope and in need of human warmth when she
addressed him without the formal use of Major.

"How?" said the incredulous Adam.

"He was found next to his car, parked in his usual spot
in the parking garage. He must have fallen just outside
the driver's door. He was on the floor between his car and
Colonel Hodge's car parked next to his. With his spot in
a corner, he wasn't discovered until noon today, when the
Colonel went back to the garage."

"Didn't someone think to check the garage earlier?"

"Yes. They sent someone to the garage about ten o'clock

167

this morning, but they only looked at his car from a distance. They didn't think to look any closer. They thought that maybe the General had some last-minute plans and just went on to that. I know that wouldn't have been like the General but ..."

"Any idea about the cause?"

"No, but everybody thinks it was probably his heart."

Adam had left Erin's office expecting that the next important thing he would hear would be from her. She would be telling him about the arrangements for their trip to San Antonio and Fort Sam Houston. Not this!

———————

The Supreme Leader had just received the news, and he was elated. Kim Il-un wanted to stir up some angst in the United States and he couldn't think of a better way to did it. Given what he had in mind, the more clouds on the horizon the better. The more his planned action would be considered just one event in a complicated world.

The agent in Washington, D.C. had been given strict orders, not directly from the Leader, but an immediate superior. And the agent had delivered. Kim always had a surrogate make the request, but the person always knew that it was the wishes of the Supreme Leader himself. The order from Kim was: find the highest-ranking official you can and give him the "treatment." Of course, that meant Kim's favorite assassination device—VX toxin. Killing the highest-ranking military officer in the United States was both brilliant and lucky.

———————

Sick at heart, Adam headed straight to the Pentagon to see if there was anything he could do. When he arrived,

Cissy had more unwelcome news. He knew things could move fast, even in the bureaucratic muck of Washington, but this was too much. He was being hit with an example of unwanted lightning speed. Air Force General Paul Lippmann had already been named Acting Head of the Joint Chiefs of Staff. This was as it should be because this important post had to be manned. The bad news was contained in a note from the Acting Chief that Cissy had transcribed as she heard it from him over the phone. The note informed Adam that his temporary assignment to the CIA as a liaison would be withdrawn immediately. His presence would be required back at the Pentagon for an indefinite period to help manage the transition.

How many things can possibly hit a person at once? He had lost a boss, friend, and mentor all in one. He was essentially being withdrawn from a vital project that was well underway, and his new boss, although temporary, was clueless of Adam's real status, but totally in command of his activity.

Erin needed to know, now. He called her cell phone and she answered immediately. "Adam, you know I haven't been able to make any arrangements yet. Is something going on with you?"

"Slow down, Erin." This was the first time he had heard this "Ice Maiden" even slightly rattled. "I just got a call that General Wieland was found dead in the parking garage at the Pentagon, probably of natural causes." He heard Erin gasp. "The first thing we have to do is somehow get word to General Lippmann. He has to know that I can't be withdrawn from our operation, and we need to do it without blowing our cover. Obviously, I am not that important, but under the circumstances he is doing the right things and if this were different I would even feel important. The truth is, now I just feel sick."

Erin, now composed, said, "I have to see Director Zinsky

about getting us to Sam Houston and to have him make arrangements for Captain Yuen to be given time off to meet us. I will ask him to get the word to General Lippmann. He will probably go through or work in parallel with Director McPherson. You have enough on your plate, Adam. I'll take care of this."

"Okay, thanks, Erin. I will wait for General Lippmann to hear about me from someone else." What Adam didn't say was that he was sorry he hadn't had a chance to talk with General Wieland about Chad Gale getting home from Afghanistan. He hadn't actually promised Brenda but he definitely left her with the virtual guarantee that her husband would get home in time. There was no way he could ask his new boss, who he wouldn't even be working for.

THIRTY

May 4, Thursday

ERIN WAS ABLE TO MEET WITH DIRECTOR ZINSKY EARLY that evening. He was an important guy, but he was approachable and down to earth. Not a stuffed shirt or a self-important bureaucrat.

"Come in," he greeted her as she entered his office. "Please, have a seat. I have been expecting you and am eager to hear how your project is moving ahead. I didn't want to bother you because I knew you were working, but it wouldn't have been long before I would have initiated this talk."

"Thank you, sir. I had planned for this meeting to be a fairly simple logistic matter. I'll get to that later, but I have some bad news."

"I know the bad news. I got it, too, late this afternoon, about General Wieland. It's awful, just awful."

"Yes, sir. It is awful, and in so many ways."

"Like?"

"You see, sir, Adam Grant's assignment to us, for three months or possibly longer, was arranged solely by General Wieland. He knew the reason, but he didn't know the details. He was leaving that up to us—you, to be exact. We know this matter was discussed with DNI McPherson and you, but who else knew, or wanted to know, was above our pay grade."

"I know most of what you are saying, Erin. How does the General's untimely death impact the project?"

"You see, sir, Acting Chief Lippmann has recalled Adam. That is not an unreasonable action if Adam were merely schmoozing while he was here; but under the circumstances, it is a disaster. I am sure General Lippmann would rescind that order if he had any idea of the importance of Major Grant's being here, but how does that message get to him without going into detail?"

"You said you were coming to see me before you heard about the General?"

"Yes, sir. I need to request that arrangements be made for Major Grant and me to visit an officer at Fort Sam Houston. The person we plan to meet is the potential defector. The Trojan horse Major Grant will be attempting to recruit. We would like to leave here as soon as possible and without fanfare." That last comment was not something even considered around this place; nothing was done with fanfare. That went without saying, but Erin was not entirely herself at the moment.

"I got it, Erin. I will get word to General Lippmann to call off the dogs. That will be easy. He may have done this simply out of respect for Major Grant. I am sure the General has his own aide already and he can move over with him. Changing gears just a bit," the Director said, "there is something I have learned at this job. Whenever I ask somebody to do something, I get the feeling that they think there is a big secret behind the request. They comply and don't ask, even when I ask for a glass of water—'what did he mean by that?' It goes along with the spy stuff. General Lippmann will be easy. And, as far as travel and arrangements for getting you to Fort Sam, we can get you there. Just give us twenty-four-hours notice and we will see to it that you two get there and have a place to stay."

"Thank you, sir. That will mean a lot to Adam, and it will to me and the team. We'd like to depart tomorrow afternoon. Oh, and there is one more thing, sir. We need a Captain John Yuen, currently teaching in the Medical Field Service School, to be assigned to one day of meetings with an unspecified group for an unspecified reason without creating too much alarm. Or, it might be better to make up a reason and switch gears when we arrive. Just tell us which way it will be."

"We can do that from this office. If we come up with a meeting topic, we will tell you in advance."

"Finally, sir, we need to figure out a way to communicate with Director McPherson. To the best of my knowledge, he has only spoken with General Wieland and you and if he wanted or needed to know any more it is likely he would have gone directly to the General. He may have stayed in close communication with the General or maybe not."

"That will be touchy. He is my boss, but I can get the ball rolling."

"I should ask you now, sir. Is there any reason why we should slow down on the project?"

The CIA Director pondered the options before answering. "The danger from Kim and, therefore, the reason for the project, remains acute and unchanged. A very important communication link has been lost, but it could be reconstituted because the number of participants is small. The team at the CIA has been making good progress and they are on target. Whatever fallout that would have to be dealt with from this project would have hit first at General Wieland, but with him gone, it will have to be the intelligence service, and maybe that is as it should be. All things considered, Erin, let's go ahead. And please, Erin, give me a 'one pager' on what we decided here. I don't want to leave anything out. By the way, I appreciate all that you are doing. I will be in touch with you as needed."

As soon as she left the Director's office, Erin called Adam. He did not answer so she left a voicemail message. "Adam, we are leaving for Fort Sam tomorrow at three in the afternoon. Call me as soon as you get this."

Twenty minutes later, Adam returned the phone call. "Sorry, Erin. I drove over to pay my respects to Mrs. Wieland. She is pretty broken up, but her kids are already on their way."

Erin explained they would be leaving from the private terminal at Andrews Air Force Base tomorrow at three, emphasizing the time in case he hadn't heard it on her message. It would be just the two of them. His clearance would be arranged and he would be picked up and taken to the military flight connection office at Andrews where he would check in for the flight.

THIRTY-ONE

May 5, Friday

THE GULFSTREAM 150 HAD EIGHT SEATS, TWO CREW, a small head, and it was fast. The air miles to San Antonio were 1,387. The Gulfstream topped out at 645 mph. Flying time would be two hours and forty-two minutes. It would leave from Andrews Air Force Base with a light passenger load: Erin and Adam. They would be landing at Lackland Air Force Base at 4:42 PM local time. They were booked at the Hilton Palacio del Rio. Not pricey, but well located.

———————————

By the time Adam and Erin checked into adjoining rooms at the hotel it was nearly six thirty. They had avoided getting too involved in the events that would be taking place tomorrow, there wasn't much to say. They had talked mostly about the city. It turned out it was a first visit for both.

"I have no idea what we should do, but I have heard the River Walk is interesting and it is located at our front door here at the hotel," said Adam. "We can take one of those pontoon boat-taxis and go up the river until we see a place we like and try some of the local cuisine, if you can call it that."

"Sounds like a plan to me," agreed Erin. "I am going to change into some shorts. I'll meet you in the lobby in twenty minutes."

The air was hot, the river murky; and the restaurants relentlessly Tex-Mex, with small tables under umbrellas pushed right to the water's edge. They picked a restaurant that was not too crowded and both ordered chicken enchiladas, refried beans, and rice. Erin had a margarita and Adam a Diet Pepsi. The place was noisy, conveniently so; they were both ready to discuss tomorrow.

"Adam, what odds would you give us for success tomorrow?"

"Fifty-fifty is where I am now, but I am willing to change those odds the minute we see Captain John Yuen tomorrow. He's not stupid. He's thinking as hard as we are right now, and he is probably deciding, do I do it, whatever it is, or don't I? We will not be in suspense long."

"What will be your opening gambit?"

"Depends entirely on what I see in his eyes. He probably already suspects something pretty big is up, and when we arrive tomorrow, his suspicions will be confirmed. If I think there is a chance of him signing on, I'll hit it hard with the truth, and do it soon. If he is the kind of person we want, he will not want to listen to us beating around the bush."

"This deal is in your hands now, Adam. About all I can do is wish you luck for the sell. I will be able to contribute once you have made the sale—but at first, it's your baby."

They were back at the hotel by nine thirty, and suddenly both realized they were dog tired. As they entered the lobby, Erin said, "Meet you here at seven thirty for breakfast."

"Okay. Sounds good."

Once he had settled on which of the eight pillows on his bed was least ill-suited, Adam crashed. As he was drifting off to sleep he thought about the pillow craze that had taken hold in the hotel industry. Each place was trying to outdo the other, but the contest seemed more devoted to quantity than comfort. Oh well ...

THIRTY-TWO

May 6, Saturday–Sunday, May 7

AFTER A MOSTLY QUIET, CONTEMPLATIVE BREAKFAST, Erin and Adam got in a cab at the hotel and headed to Fort Sam Houston. Once there, they checked in at the base commander's officer. They were welcomed and led to a small conference room on the second floor. The sergeant asked if they wanted coffee or water. They accepted the water and he brought three, knowing they would be having a third person.

At 9:00 AM sharp, a medium-height, ramrod straight, Army Captain wearing fatigues entered the room. When he had been asked at Langley about preparations for this meeting, Adam suggested that fatigues would be appropriate for the Captain. It gave a strong suggestion of soldiering and that was what today would be about.

Captain Yuen was unaccompanied. After introductions, the Captain sat at a small table, not unlike those in a police station interrogation room, he on one side and Erin and Adam on the other.

Adam began. "Captain Yuen, first of all, thanks for being here." Of course, he had no choice in the matter. He had been ordered to be here. Adam felt a little strange in civilian clothes while on an Army base, but that was the persona he had voluntarily assumed when he hooked up with the crowd at Langley.

For the next hour and twenty minutes, Adam laid out the entire scheme with the bad, the good, the dangerous, the heroic, and more. John Yuen, they were now on a first-name basis, looked on impassively. When it was time for him to ask questions, he said, "Why me?"

"As I explained, you are Korean, an Army officer, and a person with gravitas. I remember you from the Point and it was my opinion that you were the ideal candidate for a tough and heroic job."

"Must my family be kept in the dark?"

"Yes. For the success of the mission, and for your own personal safety, it is our opinion that secrecy is an absolute requirement. And, not insignificant, is the fact that there are a lot of people, including in the upper tiers of government, who are not officially aware of what we are doing. They are essentially being kept in the dark. We understand that keeping the truth from your family and friends may be the hardest thing we are asking you to do. The fact that this is the first thing you asked only reinforces our belief that you are the right person for the job."

"Would you do this?" asked Captain Yuen.

"Actually, Erin and I will be in Pyongyang for a week in advance of your part of the mission. We will be meeting with and organizing a resistance group that will work in any way they can and will be ready to take over when Kim is taken down. Any one of the assets we are to meet could be the real thing or a double agent. In case of the latter, our life expectancy will be zilch, and the mission will end there. You will be inserted only after we have determined that the operation is feasible.

"Moreover, if the mission is aborted, any U.S. involvement will be categorically denied and we will be branded rogue if we are detained. We may get private posthumous recognition, but we won't be there to enjoy it. Our parents would be notified eventually but not right away. Any level of success our effort achieves makes it all the more likely that yours will too. You will be inserted only if and when we are confident the mission can succeed. Your question was straightforward and I spent a lot of time talking around it. The answer to your question is yes, I would do it, but you are a far better candidate."

"Do you have any more questions?" said Erin

"Am I the first person you have approached about this?"

"Yes," said Adam."

"You said there are only a few people in authority who know about this."

"Yes, John," said Erin. "It is hard to explain but only a small number of people know what is really going on, although several others in the very highest offices in the government know something like this is happening. They are endorsing the actions of people they trust; that is, policy, but are declining personal knowledge of the details for the sake of plausible deniability."

"No offense to either of you, but if I accept this assignment, will I be able to speak with the highest-level person in Government who is knowledgeable and endorses this plan?" asked Captain Yuen.

"Absolutely. Do you need to know their names?" said Adam.

"No, Major I do not. I believe what you are telling me is what I need to know now. If I decline, there is no reason for me to have this information."

Pretty savvy thought, in my opinion. If he did agree, he could always back out if we didn't come up with someone like Zinsky or McPherson or maybe both, thought Adam.

"Keeping my parents in the dark is non-negotiable?" was John's next question.

"I am afraid that is the way the program is designed."

"Can I have a night to think about this?" asked John.

"Yes," said Adam. "We will meet tomorrow, right here, at the same time."

"I'll be here," said John. With that, he left.

———————————

Sitting in the back of the cab, Erin asked, "Will he tell them?"

"My guess is he will."

"Do you care?"

"No, Erin, I don't," said Adam. "And I think this is the last we should say anything about this. Are you okay with that?"

"Yes."

———————————

In the same room at 9:00 AM the next morning, the same group was positioned as they had been the day before. John Yuen was the first to speak. "I have decided I will do it. But, you must realize that I will have to start the process totally from scratch. I will need lots of help and guidance to get ready." Then after a pause, he said, "What do I do now?"

It was now Erin's turn to answer questions. "John, you will immediately be placed on assignment as a liaison to Langley. That is also Major Grant's status. We didn't mention it, but he is actually Adjutant to the Chairman of the Joint Chiefs—or, he was until General Wieland suddenly died this week."

"I saw that," said John.

"You will be assigned to Langley and billeted there. You will be trained extensively, for at least three weeks, in all aspects of the mission. This will include a period of time at Camp Peary. At The Farm," was Erin's quick comment in answer to a quizzical look on their newest team member's face.

"I learned a lot there. Your time at The Farm will be well spent," added Adam.

With that, Adam and Erin stood. "We will be heading back now. Your orders should come through on Monday. We will see you as soon as you get to Arlington. I am sure there is no need to tell you, this mission is top secret; all of our lives depend on it. You can tell anyone who asks that you are being assigned to a training mission prior to deployment—the truth but not all of it. You will be ferried up on one of our planes, and will be met and escorted when you arrive at Andrews."

THIRTY-THREE

May 7, Sunday

BOB ZINSKY WAITED UNTIL NINE O'CLOCK TO MAKE THE call. He had been fully awake and thinking about it since six, but three hours wouldn't make or break the deal. He dialed a cell phone number.

"Orville McPherson here."

"Orville, this is Bob Zinsky. I know we briefly touched on the mission, when we discussed how to handle the thing with General Lippmann, but there are some important new developments that I want to tell you about. But first, Lippmann granted my request about Major Grant, and didn't demand any further explanation. Since Lippmann will eventually pick his own adjutant, there is no big loss for anyone."

"I'm glad to hear he didn't press you. They can, you know."

"I do."

"What's your other news?"

"Our two project leaders were successful in Texas, so another important component of the mission is in place. But there is another issue that must be dealt with, a big one, before we commit to the point where we could become culpable. I don't want to go into more detail now. Can we talk before the Council meeting tomorrow?"

"Yes, I can meet, and we should. The problem is, a private meeting in D.C. is an oxymoron. Can you swing by my place by seven thirty tomorrow morning for some home cooking? That would give us about an hour before we head to the White House, and my cat doesn't talk."

"I'll be there."

THIRTY-FOUR

May 8, Monday

MRS. MCPHERSON HAD SOME SERIOUS HEALTH PROB-lems and required help for her personal needs. Bob Zinsky had met Orville's wife at social events on several occasions; she was a bright and vivacious woman, but as Orville had explained, "some of the parts are wearing out." Breakfast was prepared by a live-in maid/assistant.

"Eggs any way you want, bacon, fruit, toast, and coffee," was the way she described the morning's offering. Breakfast like this was a treat for Bob Zinsky, a bachelor.

"Where do we stand, Bob?" was Orville's opening.

"As of this minute, Adam Grant is being trained, the Langley support team is in full swing, and they will be ready for the initial launch in ten days. The Trojan horse has been recruited and will arrive here tomorrow to begin his training."

"What is the next step?"

"The two project leaders will go to Pyongyang first. With the help of assets on the ground there, they will meet with locals to confirm there is enough support from those who say they want Kim removed, and also to make sure there are enough 'soldiers' to pull it off. It is essential that they enlist a person who has the prominence and leadership abilities to at least form an interim government that can hold things together until there are elections. We have been working on this and believe we have found such a person."

"Sounds like a reasonable plan."

"We are already communicating with some North Korean leaders who want a change, but we need a rock-solid confirmation from that person who is willing and able to take charge before we insert the Trojan horse. At any time prior to the actual insertion, we can abort the mission without taking too much flack. The biggest risk in the preparation phase is that we could lose our two project leaders. If they are exposed, we will be forced to put up with North Korea's 'official' indignation. Erin O'Leary and Adam Grant are aware of the risk to their lives and they accept it."

"So, if we come up short and need to abort, there will be no real headache for the administration about what we were up to?" Orville McPherson was summing up.

"That's right," agreed the CIA Director.

"If we insert the 'horse' and he fails, we can say he was acting alone. There would be hell to pay for the people he leaves behind here, in the U.S., but the loss would be felt with or without our assuming responsibility," commented Orville.

"I know. And any possible attempt at repairing the damage would be, at best, a long game with lots of headaches—but when has international politics been anything but a long game in need of an aspirin?" agreed Zinsky.

"If we are successful, a few people will be angry; especially China and Russia, but they would find something to be pissed off about anyway; and we know, in reality, they will be happy to be rid of Kim. The major disappointment for China and Russia will be that we would have removed a thorn that has been stuck under our saddle for a long time. Of course, they can't say that out loud." Orville was looking at the bigger picture.

"To my thinking, Orville, we are on the same page and that's good for the project. The trouble is, this was Bill Wieland's baby and we were merely complicit. Now the deal is ours and whatever happens will be on us."

"I agree, Bob. I also know that if it works, our role will be essentially invisible. But if it fails, we will take whatever heat that comes our way." Thinking it was time to put an exclamation point on the discussion and to finally confront the skunk in the woodpile, Orville continued. "What all of this amounts to, Bob, is that we are doing the President's bidding without dragging him into the mess. I believe he would nix the idea if he had to take the responsibility more or less publicly, because he would not be merely speaking for himself, he would be speaking for the institution of the Presidency. Frankly, I wouldn't blame him if he did. On the other hand, I am confident he is perfectly willing, actually eager, to have it happen—for us to move ahead. But he doesn't want to know, and we simply can't tell him. This mission reminds me of Reagan and Iran-Contra."

"I suppose George Washington didn't get permission to cross the Delaware, and that turned out pretty well." This was the practical view of the CIA Director.

Both men, satisfied that they had said what they needed to say, thanked the cook for an excellent breakfast and went off to the White House and the meeting with President Tripp and the rest of the National Security Council. Bob Zinsky drove in his own car and Orville McPherson traveled in a government car with his driver.

———————————

In the Situation Room, Orville McPherson and Bob Zinsky sat on opposite sides of the table. The President opened what would be the third meeting of the group. He started with a question. It was directed at the CIA Director. "Bob, what news is there from Pyongyang?"

"Mr. President, things are heating up. Our sources are even predicting a date for a big event that involves the Leader. We don't know exactly what it will be but we are anticipating a date."

"When?"

"Our best information is pointing to Monday, June 5th, but the exact date could be shaky. It could be later, but definitely in June. We don't know if it will be the big one. We certainly hope not."

"General Lippmann, welcome to the group," said the President. "Are our missile interceptors in place?"

"Yes, sir, they are. But as you know, the ones we depend on most are able to intercept the missile only at the end of its trajectory. With that design, we put a lot of faith, really all of our faith, that we can accomplish the take down with an accurate strike in a short operational time window. At the other end, our interceptors for the lift-off stage give us more time to hit a slower-moving target in a longer time window farther from the target. They are deployed but are as yet unproven."

"Thank you, General."

"Bob, how are things going in your shop?" the President asked the CIA Director as Orville McPherson stared intently at Bob Zinsky to assess his response.

"Mr. President, we have an especially effective and

responsive team in place and we anticipate good things will happen."

Response around the table was mixed and unspoken. The look on the faces of the group seemed to ask, what in hell did he just say? The President merely thanked the CIA Director.

Orville looked across the table with a subtle smile that silently conveyed his approval of Bob's response.

THIRTY-FIVE

May 15, Monday

T HE WEEK SINCE THEIR SUCCESSFUL RECRUITMENT OF John Yuen had raced by for Erin and Adam. They were now immersed in solving the mysteries of how the miniature radios and GPS devices would operate in their minuscule forms, both during their time in Pyongyang and later in the South, when they would be supporting John Yuen. Eddie Freeman had lived up to and even exceeded his reputation as a true genius at electronics.

In Phil Park's shop, they studied the backgrounds and current status of the assets and other potential contacts Erin and Adam would be dealing with in Pyongyang. What could they expect from each? What were their strong points and what should they be wary of? Where and when would they make contact? There seemed to be a million details, which could be considered minor when looked at individually, but the professionals in charge of this preparation knew a failure, even a small one, could be crucial in the field—a matter of life and death.

Especially important was the encouraging word from Ellen Hirschman that she had been successful in contacting General Lee Wu-jin, North Korean Foreign Minister and UN Observer. He said he would cooperate fully with the coup and would assume leadership of the group of dissidents who would establish new leadership for the country. He said he was looking forward to meeting the two people from the CIA who would soon be in Pyongyang and to learn more about the details of their plan.

Not the least of the tasks that Adam and Erin faced was the need to become convincing as a clothing manufacturer and a merchandiser. They needed to know all of the properties of vinylon and the implication of the size and type of threads best for fabrication of the special garments and appliances they were pitching. How much heat would be introduced by the devices that would be inserted in their health wear and therapeutic wraps? What were the best dyes to use? And there was much more. They were confident the factory manager would be happy if the mission succeeded—but it is likely he would be just high enough on the pecking order that he might not want to take any risks that could jeopardize his comfortable position. Adam and Erin would deal with him only on a business level.

Sam Bradford was awesome. He provided Erin and Adam reams of information on the subject of clothing manufacture, completely sanitized the labeling on their packed clothing, and even switched out the suitcases; one made in Germany for Erin and one from the Netherlands for Adam.

Regarding dialect and accents, Erin was okay as a German because she had been a recent immigrant. Adam practiced speaking a deliberate form of English that was common for business people from the Netherlands. These folks spoke perfect English, in a way better than native speakers, because they put special emphasis on getting it right.

Both Adam and Erin would carry out their business in English; in Erin's case, she would also be speaking and translating in Korean as needed. Adam had memorized a few words and phrases in Dutch, but he doubted the Koreans they would be dealing with had ever even heard the Dutch language spoken and would welcome and have no suspicions about English being used.

All of their travel documents, including itineraries, were saved on their new sanitized iPhones. The information was backed up with hard copies kept in their luggage. Both had laptops that fully supported their new identities with enough background noise laboriously uploaded to make them appear to be the real deal. They would leave in two days, on Wednesday. Tonight, they would have a final meeting with Captain Yuen. To keep their time both private and personal, Erin said they could meet for dinner at her place.

"But don't get excited," Erin told Adam. "We are having dinner but I'm not cooking. At six thirty a fried chicken dinner with all the fixings will arrive from Popeye's. For our last supper, I want some old-fashioned American cooking."

The finality of this comment was not lost on Adam, but it did not require comment.

———————

John arrived at Erin's at six thirty sharp. Adam had arrived just a few minutes earlier. This was the first time the three had been together since their meeting in Texas.

"Welcome to the spy den, Captain Yuen," kidded Erin.

"Thanks, Erin. If you don't mind, though," said her compatriot, "I think I will consider myself just on loan from the Army."

This registered on Adam. Funny the different reactions, he thought. Since his exposure to the machinations of this organization, Adam felt more at home in the CIA than the Army. To each his own, he decided.

The food was delivered on time; just a few minutes after John arrived. "I didn't know Popeye's delivered," said Adam."

"They don't. But Uber does. A gal who doesn't cook has to be prepared."

Adam concluded it was hard to get ahead of Erin. Her apartment was small, but most in D.C. were. It was sparsely furnished, modern, and neat like its occupant. There was one picture of her handsome-looking parents posed with Erin in a Florida setting on an end table, an only child. A large Vasarley hung on the wall over a couch. It was easily three feet square and made up of red and dark- and light-blue squares. The picture appeared to bulge forward in the center as though it came out from the surface several inches toward the viewer. It was obviously two dimensional not three. The third-dimension effect was merely an illusion. This creation of depth was the artist's signature. Like a Louis Vuitton purse, the object was the signature. These painting, prints, and tapestries commanded anywhere from $200 to $75,000. This one was probably closer to the entry level. The cost of the piece told about the wealth of the owner. Having one on the wall was evidence of a similarity of taste regardless of price. Erin had it together when it came to modern art.

After enjoying the chicken, mashed potatoes, coleslaw, rolls, and apple cobbler, they all pitched in to clean up. Everything was paper except for the utensils, which Erin put in the dishwasher.

"Are you ready, John?" Adam tossed out.

"As ready as I will ever be," he said.

Erin wasn't going to let it go at that. In a very organized

way, she went over their communication signals, time for regular contacts between her and Adam while John was working, evacuation strategy if needed, and how they would deal with the new regime.

John was a quick study. He said he had enjoyed his time at The Farm. He was trained and would be traveling to North Korea as soon as Erin and Adam sent the okay. There was no need for elaborate preparation for John's travel. He would simply need a false ID for the flight over, and Sam could do that in a heartbeat.

Once in Pyongyang, John would resume his true identity externally, but would assume a false, and he hoped convincing, facade. All of the subterfuge with John's role would come from within. He would continue to be Captain John Yuen but instead of a loyal American, he would become a hater of the country that his Korean parents had raised him to embrace. He was more Korean, he would say, than either of his parents. He went to West Point in a vain attempt to meet their expectations but it didn't work. He felt more at home in the country of his ancestors and he was more satisfied to be in North, the country that remained purely Korean, The People's Republic, and not the South—a colony of the country he was renouncing. When John shared this with his companions, it was clear that he got it and had what it took to be convincing.

"Before you leave for Pyongyang, Adam and I will be in Seoul. From there, we can discuss the final details. We will know more after we meet with our contacts in the North. We will know the date, the time, and circumstances of the event where you will confront Kim. What do you think?"

"Sounds like a plan," said John as he stood up. "Thanks, Erin, for dinner. And thank you both for letting me be part of this. I am honored."

Erin walked him to the door.

Alone with Erin in her apartment, Adam was sorting

out his feelings in his own mind—and heart when his rev-
erie was interrupted.

"Coffee, Adam?"

"Thanks, Erin, but we both have had a long day. I better
get going. I need to drop by General Lippmann's office
tomorrow and see if there are any loose ends I can help
with. I'll call you tomorrow afternoon. Good night, Erin.
And thanks." Adam wondered if the way he said thanks
to this amazing woman came anywhere close to expressing
what he meant.

As the door closed behind Adam, Erin thought, *there
goes an amazing guy, but he really hurts*. Erin knew about
Amy from the background files she had read, which made
her feel guilty about intruding on his personal life.

THIRTY-SIX

May 17, Wednesday

ERIN AND ADAM MET AT DULLES TWO HOURS BEFORE their scheduled departure on KLM Flight 1412 to Schiphol Airport in Amsterdam. They would be in business class on a Boeing 777-200 for the seven-and-a-half-hour flight. They would be traveling under their real identities, Major Adam Grant and Ms. Erin O'Leary. For the next week, beginning with the KLM flight to Beijing, they would be transformed to Mr. Jan deFever and Frau Lisa Park. Modern German practice, they were told, was to refer to both married and unmarried women as "Frau." The term *Fraulein*, or diminutive woman, was considered archaic and was rarely used.

The flight departed on time, at 5:45 PM, with a scheduled arrival in Amsterdam at 7:20 AM local time. This was the kind of travel where you get comfortable in your seat, have dinner, and then give some serious thought to grabbing some sleep. That way, the next day has a better chance of being something close to a fresh start. That was the theory, but it often doesn't turn out that way, and it didn't for Erin and Adam.

After a typical business-class dinner with a menu that promises great things but never quite lives up to the hype, Erin was the first to broach the subject that was occupying both of them. "Can you imagine what John is going through now? Just sitting around, waiting for word from us? It must be awful for him. And I am sure it is starting to have its effect, even now, as we speak. He knows he won't get the call for at least a week but he still must be thinking about it every minute."

"You're exactly right, Erin. We're fighting the devil we know and poor John has to deal, at least for now, with the devil he can only imagine."

"Always the poet, Adam. Are you sure you're in the right line of work?"

"Not necessarily—but not because I think I should be a poet."

"Ha, ha! As if I thought so!"

This banter was followed by fitful but earnestly sought moments of sleep, until the plane landed, on schedule. As each reorganized the small amount of gear at their seats, Adam said, "Erin, we have a day to ourselves and we have to stay together, no freelancing. I'm good for anything you want to do, within reason, that is."

"Adam, there is something I want to do. Amsterdam has one of the world's great museums—the Rijksmuseum. This is my first trip here, so my vote would be to spend a half day at the museum, followed by a leisurely lunch, and then back to the airport. We can use one of the private office areas in the KLM lounge to work on finalizing our plans. It is so much easier to do this kind of work in an office setting instead of an airplane seat."

The museum was everything Erin had hoped it would be. From Rembrandt to Hieronymus Bosch, and van Gogh, the art was spectacular. The newly remodeled facility retained intimacy and quality while going to great pains to make sure the visitors' wishes were accommodated. There was also an amazing array of artifacts and other interesting displays about a country that had been a colonial and economic giant in the mid-nineteenth century but now had a GDP of just five percent of the U.S.

The "grand lunch" turned out to be Bruges steamed clams with the world's absolutely, positively, unquestionably greatest French fries that were eaten with vinegar instead of ketchup. Erin pointed out to Adam that French fries originated here and not at McDonald's. Adam already knew that but didn't let on. There were so many delicious steamed clams in the pot that Adam was secretly glad when he came upon an empty shell. It was a lot of food, but both managed to devour everything on the table but the napkins. Adam was certain that Erin had a hollow leg, or the world's most active metabolism. She seemed to eat as much as he did, but weighed sixty pounds less.

At four thirty in the afternoon, they found a small conference room in the KLM lounge that was unoccupied. They settled in for some final planning. They would have four hours to work before they started the boarding process for their flight to Beijing. It would leave at 21:30—they had agreed to be on military time.

"Where do we start, Frau Park?"

"Here is where we start, Mr. deFever." Erin pointed to two ring binders.

She described the binders as the "real fake" and the "fake real." They would have the first binder with them at all times while in North Korea as the information in it described their proposed business plan; including the number and types of garments, specifications for construction, special dye needs, heat-tolerance parameters, number of pieces, delivery time, cost, and method of payment. This binder could be shared with the factory director and his team to give them a better idea of what Adam and Erin wanted to accomplish with these dealings. The book also contained a description of their company, sample advertising brochures, and distribution plans.

The second ring binder was a study guide for their personal use only. It contained a glossary of terms, a tutorial about the retail-clothing industry, and explanations for the unique heating process that would be incorporated in the finished garments that offered therapeutic benefits across a broad spectrum. The information in this binder covered things that Erin and Adam needed to know as a natural part of the businesses they would be representing. They would explain that they had no samples, only drawings, for proprietary reasons. They would make it clear that the only reason they were in Pyongyang was to take advantage of the availability of vinylon, a fabric that was uniquely suited to their needs. They would discard binder two in Beijing by shredding it at the KLM lounge, after fully digesting its contents.

Erin took the study guide and started quizzing Adam. "What is the fiber classification of vinylon?"

"Polymer."

"How long has it been available?"

"Since 1939."

"What is its melting point?"

"In excess of 250 degrees Fahrenheit, depending on the dye that has been used."

"What is the melting point of undyed vinylon?"

"It melts as 275 degrees Fahrenheit."

"What other materials have you tried before deciding on vinylon?"

"Spandex, modacrylic, and techronda."

"Why didn't you choose one of those materials?"

"None of them can tolerate the heat or tensile requirements."

"Have you ever worked with a North Korean company before?"

"No."

"In which countries do you hope to sell this product?"

"Distribution will start in Europe, and the product will be introduced later in North America. From there, we hope to expand worldwide."

"Will the Democratic People's Republic be acknowledged in the product labeling?"

"Yes, but this is a qualified promise based on reactions to the product on the roll-out. We can't make any firm promises."

This last comment was Erin's idea. It simply wouldn't be realistic for them to promise everything the supplier wanted. They should limit what they could deliver in a manner that was in keeping with good business practices. And because they wouldn't really be delivering anything, they shouldn't be tempted to go overboard. "A sharp businessman would think something was fishy if we agreed to everything," admonished Erin.

I'll bet spies are good poker players, thought Adam.

The questioning went on for a half hour and Adam's responses were near perfect. They decided that if a question came up that one of them was not comfortable with, they would defer to their partner. And if neither had the answer, they would simply say so. Both were aware there could be set-up questions aimed at trapping an imposter and they would have to be on their guard to avoid that pit-fall. When Adam tested Erin in a similar manner, she was equally proficient.

"About language," Erin continued. "We have to be prepared for the fact that no one we deal with will be proficient in English. I will translate for you when necessary, but I am sure there will be a North Korean translator with us at all times when we are doing business at the factory. I found a Korean maid in my apartment building and have spent some time conversing with her to get back in the swing. Communication should not be a problem.

"But, and this is a big one, we have to be on guard when we speak to each other in English. There is no doubt in my mind that we will be encountering people besides the translator who understand English perfectly, but are keeping that to themselves. Anything we say in English in front of a Korean should be said with the understanding that every word we say will be heard and understood. If we mess up with this, we could find ourselves in big trouble."

"That's a darn good point, Erin."

"Okay, that's the business part. I keep wanting to call it fake, but it is definitely real. Our lives depend on us making it as real as if we needed to succeed with this therapeutic-clothing deal to pay the rent." This was Erin's reminder to herself as much as for Adam that everything was significant. "Now, for the second, dare I say 'real,' spy business. The real part for us will be working with the assets. Phil Park assured me that his contacts in Pyongyang are poised for action. They will know where we are staying and will initiate contact with us on their own schedule. We should go about our regular business with the vinylon as if that were our only mission. The Pyongyang team will find us. We are to make no attempt to seek them out."

"Your guys don't miss a trick, do they, Erin?" said Adam

both as a compliment and to reassure himself that they had, indeed, not overlooked anything.

Erin continued. "We should be encouraged by the latest news from Ellen Hirschman. She was able to speak directly with Lee Wu-jin, North Korea's Foreign Minister, using a secure communication portal. It was absolutely secure at our end." Erin was referring to Langley. "But General Lee had to take some risk. Anyway, he virtually assured Ellen he would be able to deliver the goods from his end. He did say, however, that he would reserve his final decision about the details for when he met us. As a precaution, our names have not been used. Lee assured Ellen that everything pointed to our plan being a go." This was information Erin was excited to share.

It was time for them to walk to the gate to board their flight to Beijing. They were now officially Frau Lisa Park and Mr. Jan deFever.

As they were getting comfortable in their seats, the flight attendant came through with a selection of newspapers. Adam selected the *International Tribune*. Just below the fold on the front page the headline of the article jumped at him: **Chairman of the U.S. Joint Chiefs Dies.** Reading further, the account seemed factual. It conveyed the message that General Wieland's death was originally thought to be related to a heart attack …then came the jolt. 'An autopsy was performed that all but ruled out any natural cause of death. Instead, traces of the VX toxin were found in the general's system.' The article went on to describe several incidents of VX toxin assassinations; first in London, carried out by the Russians using the tip of an umbrella, and most recently, on two occasions by minions of the Supreme

Leader of the Democratic People's Republic of Korea Kim Il-un.

From this moment, the mission took on a new challenge. Adam would be avenging the death of a fine man at the hands of a truly despicable and evil person; who in Adam's mind, had relinquished his right to live.

THIRTY-SEVEN

May 17, Wednesday

KIM IL-UN WAS AT HIS MAGNIFICENT 300-ACRE RETREAT
at Wǒnsan, one hundred and fifty miles east of the
capital city of Pyongyang. Wǒnsan was built during
the time of Japanese domination to serve as a port. That
was its principal use today, except now it was mostly for
the personal use of the Supreme Leader, whose appetite for
luxury and decadence seemed to have no bounds. In addition to the yacht and smaller watercraft, there was a nearby
airport with planes and a helicopter to serve Kim's needs.
The luxury of the place acted like a pleasure magnet, which
was almost irresistible for Kim. It both tempted and satisfied this diminutive, immature, and spoiled individual who
took immense pleasure in the surroundings and with the
people it was able to attract.

But every moment was not pure debauchery. Kim also
did business at Wǒnsan; especially the kind that he wanted

to conduct in the utmost secrecy. Such business would be transacted today.

From his perch at the helm of his yacht, Kim saw General Lee Wu-jin walking down the dock toward the *Golden Pelican*. Kim hurried from his seat and stationed himself on the first deck at the end of the aft-boarding ramp. This move was intended as an act of courtesy expressed toward the country's chief diplomat, who was essentially the second-most-important person in the government. Lee was far below the Supreme Leader, who was revered as a deity, but nonetheless on the second rung of the ladder of authority.

Today the Leader needed the support of this man to ensure that things moved ahead smoothly. Kim could act as he chose under any circumstance, but having his uncle, the Minister, with him in the venture he was planning would be a big advantage. "Hello, Uncle! So nice to see you again. It has been more than a month."

"Yes, Kim, but we both have been busy." Lee Wu-jin decided to dispense with the fawning titles; besides he suspected that this was a visit where Kim would be doing everything in his power to placate his visitor. Based on their last meeting, Lee was sure the Leader would remember that he did not indicate support for Kim's wild plans to attack the United States. Today, though, Lee's approach would be different. The change, or rather apparent change, was only strategic and was in response to communication Lee had yesterday with his friend Ellen Hirschman.

As his guest boarded, Kim beckoned Lee Wu-jin to follow him to the stairs that led to the second deck, then to another set of stairs up to the third deck. He then turned aft to an open-air seating area with several comfortable chairs and a couch. This was the fly bridge deck. A full set of controls just forward of where they were sitting comprised the upper helm, where Kim had been sitting on this fine morning; doing more play acting about running his boat.

A small, young man, round and soft-looking like Kim, was seated on the couch with his feet effeminately tucked beneath him from one side. He had a glass in one hand. It was half full of an amber liquid. With the other hand, he was feeding himself a grape. A large bowl of fresh fruit was on the table at the end of the couch. Lee recognized this fellow as the one whose head he had seen poke into the pilothouse the last time he and Kim had met. He was dismissed then, and Kim did the same now. Lee wondered if the fellow was a permanent fixture, but only for private moments.

"Uncle, I called you here today, not only as a revered family member, but as an important and influential government figure who I both respect and, at this time, I need. I need your support."

"I am, of course, at your service. What manner of support can I provide?" Lee would not be dissuading Kim, as he had attempted at their last visit. His motives were different. Instead of trying to stop Kim, which would be impossible anyway, he wanted to be in on the plot and know all of the details so the necessary measures could be taken to make sure that Kim's disastrous plan was not carried out. Lee's challenge today was to avoid being too enthusiastic and inadvertently overplay his hand, lest the Leader become suspicious.

"You are here because I have decided on how and when we will act. I respect you and I honor your experience and thoughtful manner. Having your support will mean so much to me." Kim was focused and earnest with the entreaty.

"And that would be what, and when?"

"We will send a gift to the devils in America. It will be a nuclear warhead delivered by a Losan intercontinental missile. Actually, we will be sending two. First, we will strike Denver, Colorado. Five minutes later, we will do the same to San Francisco." Kim said this defiantly and in a loud voice.

"This plan is a more ambitious attack than you described at our last visit."

"Yes, Uncle, and there is a reason. The Generals believe that only one blast will get the Americans angry; while two will be more likely to demoralize them."

"When we spoke last, you had planned a bombardment of Seoul. Is that still planned?"

"Yes and no," answered Kim. "The new plan was a suggestion from General Joo, and I think it is a good plan, but I need your opinion. We will deliver an ultimatum to the South. It will be this: make peace with the People's Republic, denounce the United States, and enter into re-unification with us as an equal partner. The South will have two hours to decide. If they decline, we will bombard Seoul and commence an invasion with 750,000 active army personnel and an additional three million activated reserves. In a worst-case scenario, North Korea will be hit with U.S. retaliation, but all of the important people will be in the South after we invade."

Lee did not think it necessary to point out to Kim how it would be impossible to move many of the twenty-six million people in the North to south of the DMZ in two hours.

"We will be safe in the South because the Americans will not launch a nuclear attack there. That action would kill too many of their lackeys," finished Kim. He leaned back, looked carefully at Lee, and tried to read his reaction.

Lee had not changed his expression and simply looked at Kim. Inside, Lee was relieved to hear this apocalyptic scenario. Any doubts he might have had about what he should do and the best way to proceed were now gone. This outpouring made any action on his part to stop this insane plan totally worth any effort and danger it foretold. With all the resolve he could muster, Lee finally responded. "Kim, what you have told me does not come as a big surprise. Your plan is nothing more than the natural progression of the glorious path first blazed by your esteemed grandfather, continued by your own father, and now it is up to you as Supreme

Leader to complete the noble work started by your glorious ancestors."

With a sigh of relief and a sublime look of satisfaction, Kim spontaneously hugged his uncle. "And now, my dear Uncle, you would like to know when?"

"Of course."

"The date set for this glorious event is just one month from now, on June 16. We had originally planned it for my grandfather's birthday, but the Minister of Culture pointed out that is already a holiday and this glorious event deserves a day of its own."

"Are all of the plans in place for the launch?" asked Lee.

"Yes, Uncle. They are."

"What will you be doing in the next month in the way of preparation?" asked Lee.

"In the next thirty days, we will make preparations for the mass movement of civilians to the South and we will place two million men and women on active duty."

"And, what is my job?"

"Uncle, all I ask is for you to support my plan and to stay close, and not disappear like you did over the last few weeks. We must be together on this," added Kim.

"I give you my solemn promise, Kim. I will be in regular touch with you and will be working with the necessary people to do what is best for our country." This last statement was possibly the only true thing Lee had said during this exchange. His interpretation of what was best for the country was not the same as Kim's.

Lee Wu-jin would be a busy man for the next month.

THIRTY-EIGHT

May 18, Thursday

THE FLIGHT FROM BEIJING TO PYONGYANG WOULD TAKE about two hours. The distance between the cities was just over five hundred miles. Adam was not thrilled at the prospect of flying on the world's only one-star airline, but there was no alternative. Nor was he happy to be in Terminal 3, where North Korean agents had carried out the assassination of Kang Bon-hwa, Kim's cousin, less than two months earlier.

Was Adam now passing by or walking on the exact spot where the killing occurred? That same bastard had caused the death of Bill Wieland; Adam couldn't get this tragic event out of his mind. What had started as a mission to prevent a deranged fool from wreaking havoc had become one of revenge and justified punishment for the cold-blooded murder of a fine man and a friend.

Adam and Erin were in seats that were arranged two and two across with a narrow aisle in between. The plane was a Russian-built Antonov 148. It had high wings with a single-jet engine hung beneath each wing. The plane was about the size of a large regional jet in the U.S. It looked like it seated about fifty passengers. It didn't make Adam feel any safer to know that even Russia had given up flying its own planes, switching to mostly Boeing and Airbus aircraft.

As they were putting on their seat belts, Adam called to mind one of the myriad facts he had assembled about this trip and their eventual destination: Air Koryo had not had a fatal accident since 1983. The airline had only four international destinations, and it didn't have anywhere near the air miles of a normal national carrier—but a thirty-four-year safety record was reassuring. More reassuring was that even a secret society like North Korea couldn't hide an air crash. If one had occurred, the world would have known. Air disasters simply can't be hidden.

A flight attendant dressed in a smart, black uniform handed Adam and Erin a copy of the *Pyongyang Times*. It was no surprise to see three images of Kim Il-un plastered above the fold on the front page. Each was a different pose of him offering a greeting, no doubt to an adoring throng of thousands—probably they were nothing more than file photos.

Erin hardly said a word on the short flight. Adam knew what was going on. She was a professional. Erin was steeling herself, or more likely she was preparing Frau Park for the performance of a lifetime, and maybe even the last performance of her life.

In the hours they had been awake on their two prior flights, Adam had shared what he had learned about North Korea by viewing hours of YouTube video shot informally and shared by several visitors who had collected amateur video, mostly on their cell phones, and also from professional news organizations. Adam was running every-thing he had seen through his mind once again.

The country they were about to enter was a mammoth charade. It was a well-orchestrated façade that, no doubt, looked more impressive in the photos he had seen than it would when he saw it with his own eyes. The capital city had tall buildings, wide avenues not quite teeming, but with a reasonable number of private cars, taxis, and buses. People on the street were adequately dressed and seemed to move about freely. Visitors who paid for a tour were treated courteously by cheerful and well-informed guides. How-ever, tourists were virtual captives of their guides. They forfeited their passports upon entry into the country and would not get them back until they departed. Visitors faced arrest, incarceration, torture, and even death at the whim of the authorities for an infraction as small as removing a poster from the wall in a hotel.

There was much to see, but visitors were exposed to only what the guides were allowed to show tourists. There was no opportunity for a visitor to leave the group or be out of the sight and control of the guides at any time. People on the street avoided eye contact and there was no opportunity to speak with a local—ever.

Children at state-run schools were well-dressed and supervised by what appeared to be competent teachers. In the schools selected for tourists to visit, the children wore uniforms and did amazing things. One video Adam saw showed a classroom with twenty identically attired girls playing a difficult traditional stringed musical instrument with great skill. It was beautifully choreographed and all for show. By decree and brutality, the country had succeeded in creating automatons.

In contrast, were gut-wrenching videos of interviews of young defectors who described a lack of electricity, homes with no heat during the bitter cold winters, children dying of starvation, and even public executions. Stealing a few feet of rope from a construction site earned a death penalty for one hapless man. His execution was witnessed by a young man who had escaped to China. Children over twelve and all adults were required to attend these public executions.

When defections from North Korea became commonplace, the government sought a remedy. The solution for them was simple: when a person fled the country, the family, for as many as three generations and even more if they could be found, was tortured and executed. This retribution could also extend to neighbors, friends, and coworkers.

Adam realized they'd be landing soon and he had better get his head around what Erin and he would be facing. With intense concentration, he concluded that humankind was endowed with a robust potential for adaptation—a requisite for survival. Existence is always in a fluid state, things never stay precisely the same. If things were bad today, they could get worse. If someone put the brakes on and life remained the same or got worse more slowly, that could be construed as good. Things might even improve. That would be very good. If the person or regime that controlled this environment was always credited with anything good and could always find someone else to blame for anything bad, they had power over the people they ruled. If not being executed was defined as a good thing, and something to strive for, and a bowl of rice once a year for a starving person was also a good thing, then the bar was so low that the ruler who held this power became absolute—especially if this power had continued for multiple generations as it had in North Korea.

The society they were about to enter was engulfed in a national Stockholm syndrome. Things were bad and only Kim Il-un, the Supreme Leader, had the power to make things even a little better—and whenever he did, he was loved for it.

The plane was in its final approach as Adam leaned over to Erin, who was quietly consumed by her own thoughts. "Erin, I've got it." This feeling was too real to address to Frau Lisa Park, but Adam promised himself this was absolutely the last time while they were in North Korea he would use Erin's real name in a public place.

"Got what?" responded Erin, glad that she was being rescued from the deep thought that was starting go around and around in unproductive circles.

"I think I understand what keeps this godforsaken place in business."

"And, what might that be, Mr. deFever?"

As the plane's wheels touched down on the tarmac and the reverse thrust activated, Adam stopped short of sharing his epiphany. The plane rolled slowly to the end of the runway and did a 180 back to the boarding gates. The terminal was small but looked new and tidy. Small for an international airport, but big enough to serve two carriers; that is, it did, until China canceled its flights. The Pyongyang Airport was plenty big enough for one airline with only four international destinations. He guessed the airport was even smaller than the one he had flown in and out of many times at Traverse City, Michigan, a town of fifteen thousand.

"What was that brainstorm you had, Adam? I mean, Jan?"

"I'll tell you later, Lisa."

———————

A few steps away from the exit of the ramp that would take them to the boarding area, a man stood, looking expectant at first and then certain when he saw the two Europeans. One ethnically of his own country. As Lisa and Jan approached, he bowed; as did a smaller man at his side—their interpreter.

"Welcome. I am Kim Tae-yong. I have only a little English and no Dutch or German," said the man who obviously was the boss. He turned to the short fellow at his side and spoke quietly and rapidly.

"My name is Kwan Sang-chu. I will be serving as interpreter. The Director was told that it would be suitable for us to converse in English."

"Yes, that would be fine," said Lisa. She then switched to Korean, telling him she also spoke his language; implying any communication that occurred in this group would always be understandable to both parties. This was both a courtesy and a warning. After this, she turned to Jan and explained that the director of the North Korean Vinylon Fashion Factory himself had done them the honor of meeting them. She knew these words would be relayed to the director when the time was right.

After they collected their luggage and cleared Customs, the four headed to an adjacent parking area. They stopped at a medium-sized SUV with Korean name plates that Kwan explained with pride was a Pyeongwha Pronto, a vehicle made in North Korea. In his studies, Adam had learned that the North Korean automotive industry was geared mostly to military vehicles. They also built trolley buses, trucks, and a few cars. There were relatively few private autos in the country, and most of them were imported. He suspected this was a company vehicle.

They were taken directly to their hotel, The Hotel Koryo Pyongyang. At the hotel entry, Kim, the director of the Fashion Factory, gave up the car to the attendant and the four entered a splendid but overdone 1970-ish-style space with a multistory atrium that was the lobby.

Jan and Lisa checked in, were given room keys, surrendered their passports to the registration clerk, and a bellman collected their luggage to deliver to their rooms.

Jan did not tip because he didn't want to take the chance of being misunderstood.

With the preliminaries taken care of, the Director led them to a small bar and lounge area to begin their business. There was no need for Jan or Lisa to be worried about the contents of their luggage, thanks to Sam Bradford. That precaution was for good reason. While they met with Kim, their bags would be thoroughly searched; undoubtedly part of a well-orchestrated plan. Kim ordered coffee for himself and his interpreter, and Jan and Lisa did likewise.

THIRTY-NINE

May 19–23, Daytime

OVER THE NEXT FIVE DAYS, LISA AND JAN PROCEEDED with Kim and his team with full effort; working through the weekend, which was treated as any other two days of the week. Their time was spent mainly with the Director and his four chief assistants, each of whom was in charge of a different area: materials, production, design, and shipping.

Initially, the hardest part for Lisa and Jan was to maintain the high level of concentration and enthusiasm necessary to carry off the act. But soon Adam found himself getting into the role of Jan in earnest. When it came to designing the therapeutic camisoles, leg wraps, and men's underwear, he was now on a roll. He began coming up with good ideas on the fly. Adam was into it as much as Jan pretended to be. *We humans are adaptable*, Adam thought.

The negotiations took less than the week they had actually planned for. After five days of intense activity, including discussions and negotiations, Jan and Lisa's work at the Fashion Factory had been completed satisfactorily. Over the course of the contractual obligation, they would purchase fourteen million individual pieces in five different designs all made of vinylon. There were four different dye lots and the special parts that must be sized were stipulated. The first goods would be delivered to the Therapeutic Garment Company in Amsterdam in August. Either Jan or Lisa, or both of them, would return to North Korea before the goods were delivered if that became necessary. The contracts were signed on Tuesday, May 23. All of their business was completed. Lisa Park and Jan deFever told Kim they would stay four more days to take part in a tour that he had arranged.

As soon as Lisa and Jan left his office, the Director called the number he found in the company literature they had given him. It had the telephone number of their company's home office. The Director asked to speak to the president. After a short wait, while his call was redirected, he was soon speaking with the Assistant to the President. Actually, he was telling Phil Park at CIA Headquarters how satisfied he was with his dealings with Mr. deFever and Frau Park, being sure to get their names in. There was no untoward reaction, and Phil assured the Director he was dealing with two of the best the company had to offer. Director Kim, now with assurance he was dealing with a legitimate company, was satisfied he had completed a lucrative business deal. Fully content, the Director slept well that night.

For Adam and Lisa, their day job was over, and it had been successful. The night job they had been working on since arriving in North Korea remained in full swing but was presenting challenges they had not anticipated. Tonight's meeting would be crucial.

FORTY

May 19–23, Evenings

O N THE DAY OF THEIR ARRIVAL, AFTER THE DIRECTOR and the interpreter had left the hotel, Jan and Lisa headed to their rooms on the 18th floor of Tower One. The building was thirty-two stories. There were the appropriate thirty-two buttons in the elevator on the call plate, but the highest number shown was for the 27th floor. North Koreans were famous for starting big things and not finishing them. The top five floors of Tower One might be an example of this. It was also said that rooms below floor twelve were plain and used for low-rent housing for locals because the hotel itself was never filled. It was possible the developers blew their budget on the super elegant lobby.

Exiting the elevator on the 18th floor, the pair turned left and found Room 1807 for Adam and Room 1809 for

Erin. They went into their own rooms after agreeing to meet in Adam's room in a half hour.

Adam unpacked his suitcase, that looked exactly as he had packed it, but he was sure it had been thoroughly searched, even though it was still locked and closed tightly. The searchers must have been disappointed. It has been said the best packers in the world are the Russians because they have had so much practice unpacking, searching, and re-packing visitors' belongings.

Before unpacking, Adam read a note that had been slipped under his door. It offered the cryptic message: "Order room service for 8:00 PM. Order whatever you want, you will get it." He suspected this was the work of the North Korean assets Phil Park had told them about. At seven there was a light tap on the door and Adam let Erin in. "We have our first contact," he said as he showed her the note.

"Are you satisfied this is the real thing and it's actually one of our contacts?"

"Yes, or I guess I should say, I hope so," said Adam. Then he showed Erin a small double fold at the corner of the note. This was a pre-arranged signal that Phil Park told him would be added to every note they would receive from their contacts. It would confirm authenticity.

"Do think there is any chance the project could fail?" Erin sounded doubtful for the first time.

"Yes, but that's not something I have any intention of entertaining. Any person can fail, and any project can go bust, but that is simply not going to happen to us or to our plan to stop Kim from accomplishing the crap he is planning. Enough of that. Anything you recognize on the menu or have any inclination to eat?"

"Yes, a few things. But how do you eat beef in a country with no cows?"

"May I make a suggestion?" Adam offered.

"Shoot."

"I heard that Bibimbap, which is a national dish, can be not only edible but also darn good. There are even restaurants in the U.S. that feature it."

"Okay, but I won't order it for the name. What's in it?"

"It is warm white rice, sautéed vegetables, and seasoning. It also comes with an egg, raw or cooked, and you can add beef."

"I can't believe you know all this stuff, Adam. Am I traveling with a true sybarite?"

"No. I just know how to use Google." Adam placed their order with a room service operator who had passable English.

At eight o'clock there was a light knock. Adam opened the door and admitted a liveried room service waiter. He pushed the cart toward a small sitting area across the room toward the window. It had a small step going up so the cart was stopped there. Ignoring the food, the waiter pulled a sheaf of papers from a pocket inside his jacket. Speaking in Korean, he said, "I am Pak. I was told to deliver this to you. It contains a list of reliable people who will be expected to support an overthrow of Kim and a restoration of freedom, peace, and progress in our country. Read this now. You will be contacted again tomorrow by another person. Thank you." With this, the man withdrew.

Erin quickly translated from the paper for Adam. The two ignored the food on the cart and instead tore into the list of names neatly printed on the paper in both Korean and English, along with a brief description of the person listed. There was also a strong admonition to destroy the paper completely, preferably by burning it, after they had digested the contents.

For the most part, the more than two dozen names on the list meant nothing to either Erin or Adam. The positions held by some of the people were impressive and encouraging. It included factory directors, but not Kim who they were dealing with, military people, government ministers, and a few professionals. One name that stuck out because it was not included was that of Lee Wu-jin the Foreign Minister. He was in a position to be at or near the highest-ranking in the country behind the Supreme Leader. Adam remembered that Ellen Hirschman referred to Lee by name, as someone she knew and trusted from the UN. Adam guessed Lee was too important to be exposed until it was absolutely necessary, at least he hoped that was why his name didn't appear. In case the plot failed, it would be better to have him available for another day.

———————

Each evening, Jan and Lisa had clandestine meetings with citizens eager for an overthrow of Kim. They were not soldiers who would take part in the actual take-down. They mostly had valuable information and pledged support for the new government that would follow the ouster.

All of this was good, but Erin and Adam were especially looking forward to their final asset meeting when they could settle on the plans for the insertion of the Trojan horse and carry out the actual deed. They were not told who they would be meeting with, but they were informed this meeting would be the most important one of the week.

A careful analysis of the information they had received to date could be summarized. There was lots of support for an overthrow by any means. That was good. Kim had made plans for a nuclear missile launch on June 16th. There might even be two missiles launched. The targets were Denver first and possibly San Francisco second. South Korea would be warned and, if they did not comply, a bombardment and massive invasion would follow. Japan would also be warned and promised safety if they agreed to terms. The news was fully as bad as they had expected. Knowing the exact time of the nuclear launch took away any uncertainty they might have had about executing their mission.

Other information was less encouraging. A very large contingent of the military was solidly behind Kim, at least with lip service. The question remained, were they loyal to Kim or did they fear an absolute monarch on whose whim they relied on for their lives? Would the apparent loyalty of these military officers melt away if Kim was no longer there? And finally, and probably most serious, reliable sources reported that the actual launch ceremony would be witnessed by thousands, with hundreds close by, and that security would be the tightest in the history of the regime. Definitely not good! Adam was sure much would be riding on decisions made at this final meeting tonight.

The directions given to Adam and Erin said they were to be at the main entrance of the hotel under the portico at 8:00 PM. A black Mercedes sedan with tinted windows would drive up. The back door would open. Nobody would get out of the car to greet them. They were to enter the car immediately.

FORTY-ONE

May 24, Wednesday

THE LEATHER OF THE BACKSEAT FELT GOOD; THE CAR smelled new. Two men were in the front looking straight ahead. The driver was younger; the passenger sat erect and seemed important, even from behind. Once they were driving away from the hotel, the passenger turned as far as he could comfortably and said, "I am Lee Wu-jin. You may have heard Ellen Hirschman speak of me. She shared with me the basics of your plan. I concur when it comes to the overall objective, but it may be necessary to make some adjustments when it comes to exactly how we carry it out. Our job now is to determine the next steps in the plan."

"Ellen did speak of you, Minister," said Erin. "And she did so with admiration and high praise."

"You don't need to flatter an old man, but thank you. We will be driving for about twenty minutes. I will leave you to your thoughts. When we arrive, we will be at my summer house where it will be private and we can talk."

After the promised short ride, the car pulled into a cedar shrub-lined driveway. After five hundred feet, it came to a halt in front of a small cottage next to a pond that was at least several acres. The architecture of the building was traditional. It had probably been built before the current dynasty, which had started seventy-five years earlier. As soon as the car stopped, three doors opened and three passengers disembarked. As he closed his door, Lee told his driver he would call when it was time for them to leave.

The main room of the cottage was austere but immaculate and faithful to the culture. At the center were four chairs around a small table. Lee offered tea that would be ready, he said, after heating water in a kettle on a small electric hot plate on a shelf next to a sink. The hot plate and sink, along with a small refrigerator under the counter, comprised the kitchen in Lee's hideaway.

With the three seated in as near to a circle as you can accomplish with just three people, Lee began. "I am sure you have read and digested all of the information supplied by the informants; as I have. What are your conclusions?"

Adam looked at Erin. Her slight nod said go ahead. "We are impressed with the apparent level of support for the overall plan we propose, but we have not yet shared the specifics. We are saving that discussion for tonight, with you. The most encouraging thing we have learned is that there is widespread discontent with the current leadership and an apparent readiness for change; and it should happen before Kim has a chance to carry out his intentions. Everyone is certain Kim's threat of a preemptive nuclear attack would result in devastating reprisal for North Korea."

"I agree that there is wide support. That is good. Do you have reservations with any part of your plan?" said Lee.

"Yes. The logistics of the launch ceremony worry both of us," said Adam. "From your description, there will be too many people. If the attempt on Kim is successful, his death in such a setting could cast him as a martyr. Having too many people witness the event could also arouse latent patriotism in people who would react out of sympathy; causing them to respond in a violent way. In that case we are afraid the project will fail and the defector we insert will be killed by an angry mob." Adam said this reluctantly but honestly.

"Do you have a viable alternative?" asked Lee.

"More of a question than a plan," said Erin.

"And what would that question be?" returned Lee.

Pleased to see this train of thought continue, Erin said, "Is there a time when Kim can be encountered alone, or nearly so, in a more or less unguarded time?"

This comment struck a sympathetic chord in Lee. "There is. If you both will indulge me, let me share some thoughts I have along that line. Kim has a very large boat. He enjoys the yacht very much. He even pretends to be driving it while it is securely tied at the dock. He also likes to be alone on the boat when it is at the dock; sometimes without his captain and always with only a skeleton of crew strictly restricted to their quarters. He also has with him a young boy who I have seen several times with him, but only on the boat. This boy seems to be doing Kim's bidding, but when I am around, Kim mostly keeps the boy out of sight. It is his business—but I expect this relationship would do nothing for the aura of masculinity that Kim says he wants to project for men of our country."

"Do you think there is a reason or a pattern to this behavior on Kim's part?" asked Erin.

"To be honest, I think Kim has a thing going with this

boy and he wants to keep it private. The yacht is a perfect place to have his fun and keep this dalliance out of sight."

"This could be his Achilles heel," said Adam.

Here we go again with the mythology, thought Erin. *From the Trojan horse to the Achilles tendon, a metaphor for Kim's vulnerability when it comes to his image of masculinity.*

In the U.S., being gay was no longer considered much in the way of a stigma. Openly gay men and women currently held important positions in government, business, and academia; and of course, in the entertainment industry. There were even gays in leadership positions in mainline religions in the U.S. and in sports. What once could be used as a basis for blackmail was now pretty close to mainstream.

"How do we proceed, based on this information?" asked Erin.

"We confront Kim when he is alone on the boat. He is never totally alone—I should make that clear. I mean to say when he has the fewest people onboard. We overcome him and anybody else who doesn't want to come along with us, and we take the boat and Kim to South Korea, dead or alive. Once there, we make an announcement to the people of the North, telling them there will be a new day—and then we pray. Dealing with him when he is out of sight will be so much less inciting than dealing with him in front of a crowd."

"When?" asked Adam.

"In three days, on Saturday the twenty-seventh of May, according to your calendar." Lee said this apologetically. The dynasty had decreed that the People's Republic calendar would honor the Mount Paektu bloodline of the Kim family by starting to count years from the formation of the Republic. In North Korea, this is now year 105, honoring the birth year of the first Kim.

Lee continued. "I will arrange a visit with Kim on his yacht, which is moored at Wŏnsan, which is one hundred kilometers east of Pyongyang, on the Sea of Japan. While we will no doubt discuss some business, the main reason for my visit will be social, just keeping in touch as Kim requested I do. It is likely that Kim will have only the minimum crew and the captain may or may not be on board. The boy, Joo, is likely to be there but he should not be difficult to manage. The overall plan will be to eventually subdue Kim, the boy, and whatever of the crew that is onboard. You will have the help of my two most-trusted men. They are loyal, dedicated, and are trained in military procedure including the close-order kind. The four of you will be in Wŏnsan ahead of time and will come to the boat when I call you. That will be after I have determined who is onboard, where they are likely to be located, and after Kim has partaken of enough alcohol to make him easier to handle. There will be five of us against what I estimate will be a total of seven or eight on the boat. We will be slightly outnumbered, but the advantage of surprise we will have and superior firepower should more than make up for that.

"When we have dealt with everybody onboard, we will then take the boat from Wŏnsan Harbor to Sokcho, which is the northern-most port city south of the DMZ. It is a distance of only one hundred and forty-five kilometers. At top speed, it will take approximately four hours. Once there, I will make an announcement on the radio and TV. Since this will not reach many people in the North, because of censorship, we will also prepare hundreds of thousands of pamphlets in the next few days to be distributed to the people."

"Great strategy," said Adam. "And now, for the tactics." Adam wasn't trying to sound presumptuous or condescending to the Minister, but he was excited as he recalled one of his last talks with General Wieland. At that meeting, the General had stressed the difference between strategy and tactics.

"Have at it, Major. I'll comment as needed," was the Minister's response. His enthusiasm was only growing.

"Minister, I don't know the layout of the yacht yet, so you tell me where we need to adjust. The way I see it, we will have two teams. Team one will be just you. You will meet with Kim on the boat and get him in a more manageable state with drink. Drunk or not, Kim will eventually be secured and locked in a stateroom with his boy; we will decide later which stateroom to use. The two will be placed in handcuffs, gagged, and securely bound with duct tape. But to start, you will decide how far ahead of time you must be on the boat to prepare Kim for out encounter. When Kim is in a manageable state, you will call on team two and we will join you on the boat, each with a specific task.

"Team two, at the outset, will be Erin, your two warriors, and me. We will travel to Wŏnsan and hole up there until we hear from you. Then, under cover of darkness, and after you have made the call, our team will approach the boat. We will disable the four or five deckhands and secure them in their quarters. Erin will immediately go to the lounge where you have told us you will be to help you keep Kim occupied. I will go to the second deck helm. If you have told us the Captain is in his quarters behind the helm station, I will confront him and give him the chance to cooperate. If he agrees, he can pilot the vessel to Sokcho. If he will not cooperate, he will be handcuffed, gagged, secured in duct tape, and locked in his quarters. Even if he does tell us he will cooperate, he will not be left alone. He will be watched constantly by one of us, especially keeping him away from the radio. With or without the Captain's help, we will take the boat away from the dock and head south as fast as the boat will take us. Under any circumstances, I will be familiarizing myself with the controls getting a better idea of how I can run the boat. Even if the Captain agrees to cooperate, he should not be trusted on his own."

Adam continued. "Before we leave the dock, Minister, you will radio the port station commander and tell him that the Leader plans to go out for an evening cruise. You will say that the boat will be gone for at least two hours. By that time, I will have assumed personal responsibility for the Captain and, with or without his help, will get us down to Sokcho. It is essential, Minister, for me to know if the Captain is on the boat and where he will be. He is likely to be our biggest challenge and must be dealt with before he can sound an alarm."

"That all sounds good," said Lee. "Erin, do you have anything to add?"

"No."

Lee then continued with his part of the plan. "You will be picked up at your hotel on Saturday at 10:00 AM. You and Erin will travel with Kwan Sang-chul and Moon Min-ho. They are two of our finest. They will both have PSS noiseless pistols and a Bizon SMG noiseless machine gun with sixty-seven rounds. They will have two extra pistols for you, if you wish to use them. They will each have six pairs of handcuffs and four rolls of duct tape. The drive to Wŏnsan will take a little over two hours. Once there, you will stay in a safe house near the port. My men will have the necessary credentials for the car to approach the boat when I call. It is likely that you will be passing one or possibly two checkpoints before you get to the boat. If I notice anything unusual about security when I pass through earlier I will alert you when I call.

"Now, let me tell you what I understand is your part, to make sure I have it right," said Lee. "My two men and Erin will go to the crew's quarters and subdue any who are there. They will be handcuffed, bound with duct tape, and locked in their cabin. You, Adam, will go directly to the bridge to deal with the Captain. If he is onboard, it is likely he will be in his quarters behind the helm. When Kim is 'entertaining,' Kim demands all crew remain in their quarters unless ordered otherwise, and this includes the Captain. When the work is finished in the crew's quarters, Erin will come to either the second or third deck aft lounge to be with Kim, me, and Joo unless Kim has already sent Joo to bed."

Adam had a general idea of the layout of a yacht the size that Lee described, but would obtain a plan of the *Golden Pelican* from Lee's men so he had an accurate understanding of the layout in order to fine tune plans.

Lee continued, "If the Captain complies, one person will stay with him at all times. If he will not cooperate, he will be dealt with in whatever way is necessary to keep him in line so we can move forward without delay. When Erin joins me with Kim, I will tell Kim I invited Erin as a special surprise and will imply that she is available for Kim in case his inclinations are what you call AC/DC. Erin and I will overpower Kim and the boy, if he is there, using handcuffs and duct tape as with the others. Then, with the help of Kwan and Moon, we will lock them in a guest stateroom. If Joo has already retired to the main stateroom, we will deal with him after finishing with Kim. When everyone has been neutralized, we will convene at the helm. I will then contact the harbor by radio and tell them we will be heading out for a short cruise. While I am on the radio, my men will cut the lines and we will depart." Then, as an afterthought, Lee said, "My apologies, Erin, if I am using you in an inappropriate and indelicate manner."

"No apology necessary, Minister. Nothing will get out of hand," said Erin.

Adam and Erin nodded. Then Adam said, "If the Captain doesn't cooperate, I have to admit you will be dealing with a truly novice captain."

"You Americans can do anything, Adam. I have every confidence that you will drive the boat expertly," said Lee.

"I think I can do it," said Adam. "But it will help if you can tell me the manufacturer of the navigation system and any other details you can find about the yacht's controls. I am sure you realize that any inquiries along this line must be kept confidential. If anybody found out, they would wonder why you are asking."

"Since your cover for Thursday and Friday is private touring," said the Minister, "you will be picked up each morning at 9:00 AM and brought back at 4:00 PM. Your tour guides will be Kwan and Moon, so you will have time to get to know each other.

"One final thing," said Lee. "How much extra expense will have been incurred by the clothing manufacturing people you were dealing with?"

"I don't know for sure," said Adam.

"Can you guess?"

"Maybe a few thousand dollars, at most."

"When this is done, we will indemnify those people as the first decent gesture by the new North Korean government," said Lee.

Classy touch, thought Erin. *And also confirmation that there is some capitalism in this Communist country.*

FORTY-TWO

May 27, Saturday

LEE WU-JIN HAD NO TROUBLE CONVINCING KIM IT WAS important for them to meet on Saturday. Lee hinted he had ideas on how to make the event on June 16th even more spectacular. During several phone calls to finalize the meeting on the *Golden Pelican*, Lee could feel the excitement in Kim's voice, and sensed that he was talking to a determined yet cheerful kamikaze pilot.

Lee arrived at the *Golden Pelican* at six thirty in the evening. The sun would not set for another three hours. The docks were deserted, which was a good sign. He encountered a guard at only one gate; he waved Lee through with hardly a glance. At the boat, he was not greeted, and there was nobody in sight. Lee knew where Kim would be. He climbed the stairs to the second deck and headed aft to the spacious lounge.

Lee found Kim sitting on a large curved couch with a

cognac in his hand; it was obvious it wasn't his first. His boy, Joo, was also on the couch, but two feet away. It looked like he was drinking lemonade. Joo was diminutive, not more than five feet two. This probably made Kim, only a few inches taller, feel more in command.

When Lee was offered a drink, without ceremony but for a reason known only to him, he opted for lemonade like Joo was drinking. Kim began talking innocently about the pleasant weather, and the sumptuous lunch he and Joo had enjoyed earlier. "The bacon-wrapped filet was sublimely tender and flavorful; the best steak I have ever eaten. (It was Kim's habit to say whatever he had last done was the best ever.) Even better," he said, "was the dessert. It was called a banana split pie but it was served in a bowl. It had a banana, of course; strawberries; chocolate chips; a small piece of pineapple; chocolate sauce; whipped cream; and a cherry on top. All of this was wrapped around rich French-vanilla ice cream." Kim, egged on by Joo, described this in rhapsodic tones.

They gave the final account in unison, as if they had rehearsed it. "This dish had just enough of everything—and not too much of anything," they said.

Then Kim added, "There should be more of this kind of balance in the world."

Staring at the two in disbelief, Lee wondered how this could be the person who was planning on killing hundreds of thousands or even millions of innocent people, and in the process cause the annihilation of his own country two weeks hence.

Once the dessert was described and after draining his glass, which was immediately re-filled by Joo, Kim got serious. He began speaking to Lee in earnest, at least to the level that his inebriation allowed. He started by asking Lee to tell him about the wonderful new plans he had for the upcoming event.

"Leader, you should just be thoroughly prepared. That is my best advice. By that, I mean you should have only those generals and technicians who you definitely trust at the launch site. You will be giving the signal by throwing the ceremonial switch in front of hundreds of thousands in the square. The launch site is miles away so you must have your best team there, because they will be the ones to actually launch the missile with the bomb, of course at your command." Lee was sure to get that in.

"A very good thought, Uncle. I knew it was the right thing to invite you here tonight." Even through the fog in his brain, Kim admitted that his throwing the switch was only ceremonial. There was no electronic connection. The actual launch would be at his signal but it would be triggered by someone else at the launch site.

I invited myself, thought Lee, correcting the chain of events in his own mind.

Kim continued. "Uncle, you are close to the military chiefs. Who do you most trust with command at the launch site?"

This question was welcomed by Lee. It was exactly what he had been fishing for. "I would strongly suggest that General Ko be given command of the actual launch. There is no more loyal man in the country than Ko. He would not be with us when the time comes, but there is no need to worry about him not being personally present at the launch ceremony."

It will never happen if we succeed tonight, thought Lee. With the official reason for the visit settled, and Kim's confidence gained, it was now time to act.

Kim's head nodded and he snapped it back up to continue the conversation that was now coming in lurches. He lost his train of thought, mumbled, and brought up a new topic. Undaunted by his inebriation, Kim continued to drink more cognac. Joo, almost floating in lemonade, said he was going to retire to their suite on the first deck. Kim offered a bleary-eyed good night to his boy and unsteadily turned his gaze back to his uncle. As the clock started to creep past 9:00 PM, Lee said, "Excuse me, dear Leader, I must use the loo."

Lee walked to the lavatories that were just forward of the lounge. Once inside, he made the call. Lee told them to come directly to the boat. Only one security gate was currently being manned, and based on what he observed, there would be no difficulty for them. The Captain was onboard and would be in his quarters behind the helm. Joo had retired to the main stateroom and would remain there if he followed the usual custom. They should move and act according to their plan.

Adam, Erin, Kwan, and Moon arrived at a small guesthouse just outside of Kim's complex a little after noon. Lee's lieutenants settled on the first floor. Erin and Adam walked up rickety stairs to a small perch of a room on the second floor, almost a loft. Both were tired, but they were so keyed up it was crazy to even think of napping.

The quartet had gone over their plans multiple times during the two-hour drive. Each knew their responsibilities. Erin had translated nonstop. It was now time for each team member to clear their heads and settle on their specific responsibilities for the job ahead.

"Is this going to work, Adam?" Erin asked again.

"This plan is significantly better than the one we came here with." Adam chuckled. "Just ask John Yuen."

Both Adam and Erin were greatly relieved that Lee had been able to contact Ellen Hirschman and tell her about the change of plans. It was even better news that she had been in contact with Orville McPherson and Bob Zinsky and that they wholeheartedly agreed with the change. And, best of all, Bob Zinsky told John Yuen of the change of plans and thanked him for his willingness to serve.

"He'll never leave the Green Room, will he Adam?"

"No, Erin. And for that, I am eternally grateful. The more I thought about this, the more convinced I became that John would die and his parents would live forever with shame. Or, if he had told them, like I am sure he did, unless he was waiting until he was actually summoned, they would live with sadness and pride only they could feel.

"I will tell this only to you, Erin, be sure I would have told his folks the truth; the hell with the establishment."

"Adam, I would have met you on their front porch," said Erin.

They both agreed, but didn't say it aloud, that if he had shared this news confidentially with his parents already, John had called them the minute he heard this latest news and that they were all having a much better day.

"When this is done, what are you going to do for an encore?" Erin asked Adam.

"The first thing I will be doing, I suppose, is looking for a job. There is no doubt in my mind I will be let go for doing all of this stuff 'off the books.' Especially with General Wieland gone and no one in the military to vouch for me, I'm dead meat. McPherson and Zinsky have bigger fish to fry. I don't think they will leave me dangling, but for sure, my time with the Army will be over." Then, looking straight at Erin, he said, "On the brighter side, at least one of us is actually doing what they are being paid for." To lighten the mood a bit, Adam referred to one of the greatest lines in moviedom: "And, frankly, Erin, I don't give a damn."

Then, a phone rang downstairs.

FORTY-THREE

May 27, Saturday

KWAN ANSWERED THE CALL BEFORE THE FIRST RING ended. Adam realized their partners were as eager as Erin and he. For the first time in a while, Adam felt like he was back in Afghanistan. He was leading this team into combat. They would not just be on patrol; they would be engaging an enemy stronghold with a frontal assault. They would have the advantage of surprise but the enemy would be fighting on familiar ground. On balance, Adam felt his team had a definite advantage. When it came to size of forces, the exact number was an unknown, but Adam was sure they could manage them without difficulty. If there were only five or six crew members onboard, as anticipated, their work could be done with stealth and possibly not a single shot being fired. That was the best-case scenario.

These thoughts swirled in Adam's head as he and Erin carefully descended the stairs. It was just after 9:00 PM. The four of them had been there since early afternoon. The long wait had only been broken by a final one-hour briefing session where each described his or her own assignment, aloud and in detail. They referred to accurate diagrams of the layout of the *Golden Pelican* they had received from Lee. When Adam spoke, Erin translated rapidly to Kwan and Moon. She was good with the language.

As she relayed Adam's words earlier this evening, he looked at her with a sudden and profound feeling of softness. This was a brave, smart, dedicated woman he realized he cared for. He didn't want to lose another.

They would board at the aft gangway and split into two and then three groups: Kwan, Moon, and Erin would go to the crew's quarters, forward below the main deck; then as soon as things were settled there, Erin would go to the lounge on the second deck aft; and Adam would go directly to the helm on the second deck forward. Kim's boy would be forward on the first deck in the main stateroom and pretty much removed from the action. He could be dealt with later. Lee would be alone with Kim. When Lee called, he said Joo had left the lounge and was headed to the main stateroom. Erin would join Lee and Kim in the lounge, and after Kim was managed, she would go to the stateroom to deal with Joo.

That meant four stations and eventually a team member for each. It would be necessary for Erin, possibly with Kwan's help, to get to Joo's room as soon as possible in case the boy realized something was amiss. The disposition of manpower would also depend on how long it took each to complete their task.

Joo would likely be sober and could sound an alert if he thought something was wrong or, more likely, he would be paralyzed with fright. This uncertainty worried Adam but it was something he would have to deal with.

The four immediately got in the car. Kwan drove. It took only ten minutes to reach the first gate of the compound. At the gate, Kwan must have said the right thing because the gate swung open immediately. Adam hid his face as they drove past the guard but he could see the guard's grim countenance. The security men closest to the Leader were probably picked for their loyalty and nastiness and not for their brains. The second gate was at the entrance to the wharf. It was open and wide enough to accommodate a car or a medium-sized truck. The gate was unattended and there was no one in sight. The *Golden Pelican* could be seen ahead docked at the wharf. Adam could see it was secured by a hawser stem and stern and two lighter spring lines fore and aft. He was glad the Koreans had sharp machetes to dispatch the lines. There would be no time for a ceremonious untying when they left the dock tonight.

At the boat's aft gangway, they stopped the car, collectively took a deep breath, and quietly quit the vehicle. The four walked up the gangway and split.

Moon and Kwan crept forward. Kwan led the way. They were both wearing black canvas shoes with thin rubber soles, a style common in the country and perfect for the task this evening. According to the diagram, the crew's quarters were forward. At the bottom of the stairs and through a door there were four doors, two on each side, that accessed larger staterooms used by higher-level crew, the people who would manage amenities dealing with Kim and his guests. All were empty. This part of the crew no doubt had worked earlier, through dinner, but now was enjoying time off.

Just forward of this set of rooms, in the bow, were quarters for the deckhands. They slept in sets of upper and lower bunk beds. When Kwan and Moon reached the bulkhead separating the quarters, Kwan burst inside, brandishing his automatic weapon. Immediately, five heads appeared. Four had been playing a dice game on a small table at the end of the room and a fifth stuck his head out from an upper bunk.

With an order for silence, all was quiet. The five scrawny men were just over five feet tall. It had been said that Kim did not hire crew members taller than he. From the looks of the men, this appeared to be true. The brawny duo of Kwan and Moon would have had no difficulty overcoming these men with their own hands if necessary, but that was not the case. The fearsome automatic weapon held by Kwan made the crew freeze instantly.

The compliant crew members immediately fell to their knees. Moon placed sturdy handcuffs on each as the men placed their hands behind their backs. They then placed a duct tape gag over the mouth of each crewman and the same tape was then used to bind their hands and feet. Kwan spoke quietly to the men as they were being trussed, reassuring them they would not be hurt and that if they cooperated, the tape would be removed soon. A sixth crew member remained silent in a lower bunk in the forward part of the cabin, undiscovered.

In the second-deck lounge, Erin encountered Lee standing over a bleary-eyed and confused Kim. There was no time for games. At the sight of Erin, Kim reeked of helplessness and terror. He was a cowering ball of fat. Erin put handcuffs on Kim and left the tape with Lee to finish the job of trussing. She headed down one deck and forward to the master stateroom. Entering the huge space that looked like an apartment, she saw Joo, who was languishing in the bed. His expression changed from sensuous anticipation to terror when he realized it wasn't Kim but a warlike woman who had entered. He muttered a few muffled sounds, but within seconds was subdued. Lee entered in time to watch as Erin put handcuffs on the hapless boy. Lee then finished trussing and gagging Joo with duct tape.

With both of their charges out of commission, to the point they could be briefly left unattended, Lee and Erin departed for the bridge. When they arrived, Adam was standing next to the Captain. Neither spoke. The body language of the Captain suggested he was giving serious thought to which of the implied options he was going to choose. When he saw the Minister, his eyes brightened. He would want to be on Lee's side, whichever one it was. Then Moon and Kwan burst onto the bridge to report that their part of the operation had been successfully completed.

With only seconds to collectively enjoy their success, a scrawny sailor with a very big gun stepped out of a lavatory located behind the helm. The event had suffered a serious setback and they were in trouble now.

There were four of them plus the Captain on one side of the helm station, which was at least twenty feet wide. On the other side, the crewman brandished a large semiautomatic weapon that only accentuated his small stature. He had positioned himself as far away as he could on the bridge, keeping the five on the other side of the room covered with his weapon. Adam guessed the type of semi-automatic Russian weapon he had could empty its clip of sixty plus rounds in as little as forty-five seconds. That would be a lot of lead in this small space. If this fellow pulled the trigger, Adam knew at least some of his team would go down before the crewman could be overpowered. There were two wild cards: the Captain and the Minister.

Seizing the moment, Minister Lee began to speak with the sailor in calm and reassuring tones. Erin whispered in Adam's ear that Lee was offering the sailor a reward for helping, and not just freedom from tyranny but also a monetary reward that could set him up for life. "It was hard to tell," she whispered, "whether Lee was making any headway but at least the man wasn't shooting, at least not yet."

He didn't look very bright, Adam thought. *In a situation like this, that could be good news or very bad news. Which would be the case here?*

Suddenly, the Captain broke free from the group and lunged toward the sailor holding the gun. Had he chosen sides?

In an instant, the sailor pulled the trigger and a single shot hit the captain in the forehead. There was a splatter of blood and brains from a gaping exit wound at the back of his head. A split second later, Moon, who had been cradling his pistol, shot the sailor in the chest with three rounds, knocking him backward. As the sailor fell, his hand, in a dying grip, pulled the trigger and a roar of bullets ripped open the head liner and pierced the fiberglass leaving a dozen holes. In another instant, Moon grabbed the gun from the dying sailor.

The once tidy room was now carnage. The Captain lay face down with the back of his head nearly blown off, the sailor gurgled blood from his mouth as he took his last breaths, and the head liner hung in shreds. A fortunate quirk of the sailor's gun was that it went on automatic only with the second pull. Adam remembered that this was a low-level safety he had encountered on some of the Russian guns they had collected in Afghanistan. This feature had saved the lives of some, or possibly all, of them tonight, except for the Captain.

Adam kicked himself for not remembering this feature sooner. He didn't like the concept "no harm, no foul." Warriors shouldn't overlook anything.

FORTY-FOUR

May 27, Saturday

KWAN DRAGGED THE BODIES FROM THE BRIDGE AND put them in the Captain's quarters. Then he and Moon took machetes to the deck and cut the lines. Adam was now the pilot of a boat one hundred and ninety-nine feet longer than the largest boat he had ever driven. That boat was a forty-two-foot Bertram flush deck motor yacht. In spite of the difference in size, Adam realized there were just three basic functions when it came to driving a boat of any size: propulsion, steering, and navigation. Under normal circumstances, a pilot's biggest concern was to avoid being clumsy and bashing the boat into the dock, or hitting another boat when operating in close quarters. All of this was off the table now. Adam's grades would be only for seamanship and survival; there would be no style points awarded or sought when it came to leaving the dock.

Erin stood by Adam as he surveyed the vast array of dials and levers. "You will have to be my right-hand man, Erin."

"Aye, aye, Captain," she said.

"Have you ever done anything like this before?" asked Adam.

"You mean steal a mega yacht, kill two people, and race through the Sea of Japan with the North Koreans in hot pursuit? No."

"I mean steer a boat, or anything useful like that."

"No," she said. "The closest I have ever come is just being a passenger, like I am now."

That settled it for Adam. He would be relying on Erin's native intelligence, which was considerable, and not her nautical experience. He found the engine start switches and activated all four of the huge diesels. They responded promptly. Under ordinary circumstances, he would allow for a warm-up period to make sure the engines were fully lubricated before increasing the RPMs. This precaution avoided excessive engine wear and added life to the engine. This could take as long as several minutes with big diesels like the *Golden Pelican* had. Adam would dispense with this nicety tonight.

Adam wanted four hours from this boat; after that, he didn't care. He would advance the throttle as soon as he felt the engines were warm enough to avoid conking out and stalling when they first had to strain. He turned on the radar and the global positioning satellite instrument, GPS, for short. Fortunately, the GPS and all of the other dials, gauges, and directions on the helm were in English. Boating at this level was much like flying a plane—regardless of the language spoken by the crew, the controls and oral navigation directions were in English. The paper charts were in Korean, but Adam would be relying entirely on the GPS for navigation tonight. This instrument also acted as a speedometer (knot log) and depth finder. The radar would tell him what was nearby in real time, including other boats on the move. The GPS would indicate their exact location in real time on a pre-loaded chart but would not register other traffic or any variations from the chart they would be using. To get away from the dock he would need the fore and aft thrusters to move the boat sideways—but where were the controls?

Lee re-entered the bridge. Where had he been? Adam suspected he had been vomiting; he had been. Now belying any tension or concern, the Minister was on the radio speaking with the harbormaster. It was obvious he had scouted out the radio ahead of time because he used it well enough to get his point across. He explained to the harbormaster that Kim was taking the boat out for at least two hours to please some guests who had come aboard. This message would serve a double purpose. It would help explain the second car and the four entering the boat if anyone had observed them, plus it would give them a two-hour head-start. Two hours had been agreed upon to avoid raising suspicion at taking the boat out this late at night.

Lee was sure that after two hours, on the dot, the har-bormaster would radio them. When the *Golden Pelican* didn't respond, and it wouldn't, speedy patrol boats would be sent out. Their speed would be in the range of thirty-five to a maximum of forty-five miles per hour. With a two-hour headstart, the *Golden Pelican*, at twenty-five miles per hour top speed, would reach the 38th parallel, eighty miles away, just ahead of the pursuing craft. Adam's mind was process-ing knots, miles per hour, kilometers, and miles seamlessly. He just wanted to get to the 38th parallel as quickly as possible.

In exactly two hours, Lee would contact the South Korean authorities and tell them of this defection. He would say they had an important passenger onboard but would not reveal it was Kim. Lee would tell them that they were being pursued and were requesting escort into Sokcho Harbor, or even better, they suggested that they would welcome a pilot coming aboard.

As Lee delivered his message, Adam frantically searched for the thruster controls. Then he saw two unmarked toggle switches below the main synchronizing throttle. He guessed that the toggles were used to turn on the thrusters' electric motors. He threw the switches and a slight whir from the motors indicated he was right. Below the toggles were dials that could be rotated right or left from a center line. These he suspected were to regulate the direction and force of the thrust. So far so good. The farther the dial was turned, the more the thrust. With these now located, it was time to move the mammoth ship away from the wharf. He would have to control the thrust so that it was equal, resulting in the boat moving directly sideways away from the wharf, without either the bow or stern getting ahead. This maneuver was necessary to get the boat far enough away so that when Adam swung the helm hard to port, the stern would not smash into the wharf. Since the boat was tied up facing away from the harbor opening, it would be necessary to swing the boat 180 degrees pointing it in the opposite direction.

Getting the *Golden Pelican* away from its berth would have to be done in a reasonably competent manner. There was no doubt the departure was being watched by the harbormaster and if things went too far awry he would wonder why and possibly raise an alarm. When the swing had been completed successfully, even if it wasn't done elegantly, Adam was relieved. This boat was a long dude. Even giving himself twice as much room as he thought necessary, the stern of the boat just cleared. Adam could see the channel leading out to the Sea of Japan. Once through the harbor inlet and one right turn, they would be on their way.

In the harbormaster's office, the two men manning the station observed the *Golden Pelican's* departure. "A different way of leaving the dock for the Captain," said one. "He is not usually so clumsy. Should we call him and kid him about his unstylish departure?"

"Don't be silly. That maneuver was undoubtedly the work of the Supreme Leader, who fancies himself a bit of mariner. If you call and give any hint of ridicule it will be the labor camp for you," said the second man.

"Right. You might have just saved my life."

They both chuckled.

Once clear of the channel, Adam headed south. Ordinarily, he would have followed a compass, but traveling close to the shore like this was different. With the GPS on a five-mile range, he observed the shoreline to starboard and just followed it. The radar, at a ten-mile range, revealed no moving objects suggestive of a boat. They were alone, traveling south at twenty-four knots, just over twenty-five miles an hour, meaning they were less than four hours from freedom.

Bound and gagged in one of the starboard guest staterooms, Kim was between sleep and stupor. Joo was with him; his whimpering was so loud and annoying there was a danger of him rousing Kim. The boy was moved to a second-deck lounge while similarly bound and gagged. The frightened crew was in its quarters with a now benevolent Moon overseeing.

As Adam stood at the helm, he thought, *We will never know what was on the Captain's mind when he bolted across the room to confront the gun-brandishing sailor. Was he a hero or was he changing sides to join the guy with the biggest gun?* Adam liked to think the Captain was doing something heroic; for the sake of his memory and his family, Adam hoped Lee agreed.

After two hours at sea, the expected happened. Realizing the *Golden Pelican* had not returned when scheduled, the harbormaster radioed the boat. No one answered. Knowing from radar that the yacht was heading south at what appeared to be full speed, with a two-hour headstart, a light plane was dispatched from the Wǒnsan airport to search for the boat. At this time, Lee went on the radio and, using the hailing channel, made the request for air support from the South. Of course, the North could hear this conversation, but by now it was no mystery what they were up to. Something was seriously amiss on the *Golden Pelican*.

Adam looked at the GPS screen, willing the 38th parallel and South Korea to appear. He felt like a slot machine player yearning for three cherries, or whatever indicates a jackpot. He could see four radar blips less than ten miles astern and gaining. *Their damn boats are faster than we anticipated*, he thought. Then it appeared. The GPS, now on a long-range setting, indicated Sokcho Harbor less than twenty miles away. The radar blips behind him stopped gaining and suddenly disappeared from the radar screen. They were replaced by three distinct blips on the screen ahead of the boat; they were approaching from the south.

In less than ten minutes, the first of the South Korean coastal craft was clearly in sight. The radio, which had remained on the hailing channel for incoming traffic, crackled. Lee grabbed the hand mike. A South Korean identified himself and requested the same. Lee did his best, but not in the nautical manner. He told them they were from the North, carrying an important passenger, and were seeking asylum. This was acknowledged.

At this point, Adam took Erin aside and said, "Erin, it is time for an executive decision. As captain, I will make it, but only with your approval."

"What in the heck kind of captain are you, making an executive decision and then asking advice?" she responded.

"A smart one. Erin, we have a lot on our plate right now, and to be honest, we threw away the script a long time ago."

"Agreed."

"Here is what I propose. We turn this whole operation over to Lee. He calls the South Korean boat and requests a harbor pilot. He can say he is not an experienced seaman, which is an understatement, and though he brought the boat down in the open sea he will need help entering the harbor. At this point, we totally check out of the picture. This is a purely North Korean operation. The United States has no culpability."

"No bows for us, Adam."

"How about we just share a high five, my dear?" And they did.

FORTY-FIVE

May 27, Saturday

ADAM AND ERIN TOLD LEE ABOUT THEIR PLAN TO DIS-
appear. He understood. Because of the urgency of
the situation, he felt he had no time to thank them
properly for all they had done, but he vowed that would be
accomplished. "Just help us get out of here and back home
quickly and quietly," said Adam. "And, thank Kwan and
Moon for us. They were great guys to work with."

Adam and Erin stole down to the crews' quarters below
the main deck. They approached the first area that was for
the higher-level crew, and entered one of them, a small, pris-
tine room similar to what would be expected in a budget
hotel in Manhattan. In addition to a double bed, it included
a small chair, built-in vanity, and a private bath and shower.
The bed was fully made and appeared to have clean sheets.

"If this is okay for you, I will check out the room across the hall," said Adam.

"No way, Jose," was Erin's response. "We're bunkin' here cowboy."

"If you say …"

Before he could finish, Erin had grabbed him and kissed him full on the mouth. In a combined effort, they both tumbled onto the bed. After a frantic rearrangement of clothes, they did something they had both been thinking about for a long time. After a short sleep, from total exhaustion, Erin opened her eyes first and said, "Was it …?"

"Great? Yes! And the foreplay started when I spied you across the great seal back at Langley."

"I'll bet you tell all the girls that."

"No. I've been waiting to find someone like you for a long time—and I can hardly believe I'm so lucky."

———————

Lee was conflicted. He was deeply grateful to Adam and Erin. What they had done so far was amazing. But he also realized the job was not finished. It had only begun. To be successful he realized that the removal of Kim had to be viewed as the result of a popular uprising and not something done at the bidding of a foreign power. It would take months and even years of re-educating to get across to the people of North Korea the true nature of the cruel dynasty they would be overthrowing.

He would honor their wishes. As soon as the *Golden Pelican* was tied up in Sokcho, he would explain to the authorities that the two Americans on board should be removed quickly and quietly and allowed to return to the United States immediately and without comment. Keeping them essentially invisible, he would explain, is of the utmost importance to the success of the project. Anticipating the relief that would be felt by the South Korean government, Lee was confident the authorities would comply.

———————

Before boarding their plane at Seoul International Airport, Erin called Langley and asked to be connected with John Yuen. She knew he had already been informed about the change in plans but she wanted to briefly fill him in about what had happened and thank him for all he was prepared to do. She promised him a detailed "blow by blow" when Adam and she returned. Erin could sense his mixed feelings "John," she said, "the guts you showed when you signed on and the agony we have put you through while you were waiting are far more significant than anything we did. And, honestly, none of this would have been accomplished without you. Now, Adam wants to say something."

"John, thank you for all that you have done. We belong to the same grey line and I know you would have done everything I did and even more if you had been in my shoes. To be honest, I got to spend a week with the coolest lady I know." This occasioned a stiff jab in the ribs from his companion. "Hang in there, John. We will see you soon. You deserve to hear the whole story—for your ears only."

Erin apologized for the poke and said, "Let's go, Major."

FORTY-SIX

June 1, Thursday

Adam and Erin were in the Oval Office. The only other person in the room was President Phillip Tripp. The floor was his.

"Erin O'Leary and Adam Grant, your country owes you more thanks than I can even express. All of us are in debt to both of you for your service. You almost singlehandedly did something that may have saved your own country and possibly the world from an unspeakable nuclear disaster. I can't even find the words to say how grateful we all are. I hope you understand this.

"I have spoken," he continued, "with Minister Lee Wu-jin and he told me the amazing things you did and the bravery you both showed. We did not have the chance to go into very much detail, but from what he said, the accounts that both of you provided don't give you two nearly the credit you so rightly deserve. Minister Lee also told me that Kim Il-un is now in secure custody in the North. With him out of power, the support for a new form of government that is truly democratic has been overwhelming. However, we have to realize it will take time for this to sink into the North Korean population. They have known nothing but a duty to worship a near deity for three generations. Lee assured me that with enlightened leadership and the obvious benefits derived, people will support a leader who will allow them to enjoy living in a free society. The North Korean government will undergo a monumental transformation soon.

"Additionally, the impact of this event has had a unifying effect, bringing together most of the countries of the world. With both China and Russia cooperating, the UN has launched an initiative to collect ten billion dollars for North Korean aid. This money will be available on the condition that North Korea does the following: immediately dismantles all offensive nuclear devices, reduces its military budget by ninety percent and limits its role to border protection, begins nutrition and feeding programs for the population, and ceases operation of all labor camps and incarceration facilities for political prisoners.

"Also, many nations will find ways to engage North Korea in an economic and trading process and help the country become a respected member of the family of nations or, better yet, accept unification with the South. The United Nations Security Council will grant the country an aggression-free treaty, sanctioned by the organization, as long as they remain independent and comply. The countries of this council pledge to defend this country from any outside aggression. Then, after North Korea completes negotiations with South Korea for the purpose of establishing mutually agreeable terms for re-unification, North Korea will only be a chapter in history. The net result of this whole affair is that the greatest destructive force known to man, nuclear power for war, can also become the greatest instrument for bringing about peace. You two really started something!"

Both nodded, somewhat embarrassed. They didn't need all of this but they were secretly happy that he knew the truth.

"The hard part," continued the President, "is you are both going back to your lives as though nothing happened. This is how it must be when you deal with people on the outside. Erin, you will go back to the CIA. I would not be surprised if it would be as a station chief. Adam, you belong to a much more rigid organization. Nobody in the Army has any idea of what you have done or, frankly, where you have been. There is no record of any orders or directives and General Wieland is no longer here. The CIA Director and the Director of National Intelligence must deny any knowledge to avert the serious consequences that would be suffered, both in our own government and with other cooperating governments worldwide. This is especially so with those who took secret pleasure while North Korea was poking us in the eye. Our denying any responsibility for U.S. involvement publicly is necessary to show this action was entirely North Korean. You have not only saved North Korea, you have also saved the United States."

"I understand, sir," said Adam, wanting to relieve the President from saying what he felt he had to but was finding difficult to put into words. "I may have had enough of Army life anyway. Can I give your name as a reference for my next gig?"

"You certainly can," said the President, thankful that Adam was making things easier, "but you realize, I can't say why."

Adam knew what he still had to do. It had been gnawing at him for weeks. Looking directly into the President's eyes, Adam said, "Sir, I have just one favor to ask."

Before he could continue, the President said, "If it is in my power, Major Grant, I will do whatever you ask. I owe it to you."

"It is this, sir. I am more or less looking after the pregnant wife of a buddy who is in Afghanistan on his second tour. He is expected to return in time for the baby, but the timing will be close and ..."

"Stop right there," said the President. "As you know, I am Commander in Chief. What is your friend's name?"

"Major Charles 'Chad' Gale."

"When is the baby due?"

"In September, sir."

"As I recall," said the President, "my wife liked having me around for the last couple of months, especially with number one. Major Gale will be stateside in July and we will see to it that he is assigned to a post here in D.C., at least until the baby comes. In this job, a fella can do a lot, but I don't think anything could give me more pleasure."

"Thank you, sir."

As Adam and Erin left the White House, it was difficult and felt unnatural for them to say good-bye. The last few weeks had been a lifetime for both and the answer to an unasked question they had yet to voice would be YES. They had both found someone, in each other.

EPILOGUE

A week later, Adam and Erin were on Lake Michigan aboard a forty-foot Nordic tug with no name or hailing port on its transom. At the dock, looking pretty much like a traditional tug boat with a deep-green hull and off-white superstructure, this sturdy craft was a thoroughly modern cruiser. In essence, it was a comfortable, two-bedroom, sea-going apartment. Built in Bellingham, Washington, shipped by truck to Manitowoc, Wisconsin, it would soon be on its way from Lake Michigan to a new owner in Florida.

A happy and expectant Adam and Erin left Harbor Springs, Michigan, on the northwest tip of the Lower Peninsula, just forty miles from the Mackinaw Bridge, at 8:00 AM. They were beginning a wonderful three weeks of furlough. It was hard to believe that during the hundreds of hours they had spent together, planning and carrying out the mission, they had shared so little that was personal about each other. Now, with just each other and no demons to avoid, they were ready for a time of pure pleasure.

The first day they went under the great Mackinaw Bridge and continued on to spend the night at Port Sanilac on the Lake Huron side of Michigan's thumb. By day three, they were docked at Port Clinton, queued up for a starting spot to go through the Welland Canal. Adam explained that going through eight locks was preferable to going over the four-hundred-foot drop at Niagara Falls in one fell swoop. Because the lift in the locks at Welland was large, thirty feet and more, and the canal was primarily for larger ocean-going freighters, Adam hired a temporary crewman for the eight-hour trip.

Their hired crew, a local firefighter who did this as a hobby, managed the bowline; Erin the stern; and Adam was on the throttle as they all worked to keep the boat secure at the wall while the water swirled out and they descended the thirty feet or more in each lock. Their new crewman also negotiated with the lock tender, getting him to open the lock even when they were the only boat instead of making them wait an hour or more for a second boat to lock through. Their helper was a nice guy. At the end, they treated him to a dinner of hot dogs and beans. He thanked them profusely. His enthusiasm had to be more for the gesture than the food, but his reaction was just another pleasant memory of an altogether pleasant trip.

"Nice, Canuck, aye?" Adam said to Erin, who had also noted that their crewman had ended nearly every sentence that way.

Along their journey, Erin told Adam about the pluses and a few minuses of growing up with mixed ethnicity. If there was any stigma, it had totally gone away. With a laugh, she said, "One thing I would do differently is have my name be Smith or Johnson, something that didn't offer the promise of a name like O'Leary; especially with a first name like Erin. Were you disappointed at my not being the colleen my name promised?" She already knew the answer but she wanted to hear it.

"Hell no, and you know it!"

Erin told Adam that her parents, both doctors, probably had her just to prove they could procreate. "I think I would have enjoyed having a brother or a sister, but I think with me they had proved a point and I don't think they wanted the responsibility of more than one child. Am I being too cynical?" asked Erin.

"Your life, your call."

"My early life somehow made a career with the CIA almost a foregone conclusion. I spent a lot of time alone or with caregivers. I may be destined to be a lifer at this. But that may be only a rationalization that I come up with because I don't have any other plans at this time. I can tell you, though, at this very minute, I am happy and satisfied just where I am. Thanks in large measure to you, Adam. I learned a lot from you."

They traveled through the Eerie Canal a hundred miles at five miles an hour. At Lock 21, the first night, they grilled steaks on shore while tied just past the lock. The next night, they tied up at Amherst, New York, and walked three blocks to an Italian restaurant, where they had dinner next to the Amherst High football team that was eating there at its night-before-the-game dinner. The next day, at noon they turned right after descending in Federal Lock 2, which is actually the first lock from the Hudson River. Lock 2 is a series of five chambers that dropped their boat 169 feet in a half mile, the largest vertical shift in the shortest distance of any lock in the world. A very excited Adam shared these facts in detail with Erin as they threw away the gloves they had used while dealing with the heavy lines in the locks.

This was a ritual Adam explained, but Erin said she would have preferred to keep the gloves for a souvenir.

A few minutes after they completed the descent and turned south to travel down the Hudson, Adam said, "It's strange going by West Point. Look, it's right over there." Adam smiled as he pointed to the riverbank dense with trees that actually hid the academy from sight.

There wasn't much for Adam to share about his childhood. He was a normal, pre-programmed, Midwestern boy. He did okay at just about everything he tried. He told Erin about Amy. He also said that he had just now started to live his life again. In a tender moment, he told Erin that she was the reason why.

After crossing mid-Florida on the Port Lucie Waterway, Lake Okeechobee, and the Caloosahatchee River, they arrived at Fort Meyers. From there they went into the Gulf of Mexico traveling up to Sarasota. Adam did this to avoid the intercostal which he was warned had abundant and shifting sandbars that made operating a tow boat much more attractive, not to mention lucrative as compared to a full keel boat with nearly a five-foot draft. They spent their last night on the boat tied up at the Mooring Marina on Longboat Key, saying good-bye in as many ways as they could think of.

Adam had to admit it. He had been with this woman, in person or in his mind, every minute for the past six weeks. They had traveled halfway around the world; taken down a rogue government; and, in a few hours, they would each be on their way, alone. On the way to the Sarasota Airport, where Erin would catch a plane to Miami to see her parents before going to her new post in Rome, Adam said, "I got a call when you were in the shower."

"And?"

"Bob Zinsky wants to see me when I get back to D.C. He called me Colonel. When I corrected him, he said he was right; and that the President told him there was more good news waiting for me in D.C."

At the airport, before Erin approached the security checkpoint, Adam took Erin into his arms. "I love you, Erin."

"Me too. I mean, you, not me." Erin giggled like a schoolgirl.

"See ya," they said in unplanned but perfect unison.

ABOUT THE AUTHOR

E UGENE M. HELVESTON, MD, is emeritus professor of ophthalmology; founder of the section of Pediatric Ophthalmology; and former Chairman of the Department of Ophthalmology at Indiana University School of Medicine, where he provided patient care and teaching, and carried out clinical research. During his career, he taught in forty-five states and also served as a volunteer surgeon and lecturer in fifty countries. In 2002, he founded an award-winning international telemedicine program to serve doctors and their patients in developing countries.

After authoring hundreds of professional papers and three medical textbooks, he turned his attention to writing about getting the best education for the career you want and working at a meaningful job starting at an early age. In 2016, *The Second Decade: Raising Kids to be Happy, Self-Sufficient Adults through WORK* was published.

A native of Detroit, Michigan, Gene currently resides in Indianapolis with his wife, Barbara. This is his first published work of fiction.

You may contact him at ehelveston@msn.com.